high-wire summer

high-wire summer

Louise Dupré

Stories Translated by Liedewy Hawke

Cormorant Books

Canada Council for the Arts Conseil des Arts du Canada

ONTARIO ARTS COUNCIL
CONSEIL DES ARTS DE L'ONTARIO

The publisher gratefully acknowledges the support of the Canada Council for the Arts and the Ontario Arts Council for its publishing program. We acknowledge the financial support of the Government of Canada through the Book Publishing Industry Development Program (BPIDP) for our publishing activities.

Printed and bound in Canada

NATIONAL LIBRARY OF CANADA CATALOGUING IN PUBLICATION

Dupré, Louise, 1949–
[Été funambule. English]
High-wire summer/Louise Dupré; translated by Liedewy Hawke.

Translation of: L'été funambule.
ISBN 978-1-897151-53-2

I. Hawke, Liedewy II. Title. III. Title: Été funambule. English.

PS8557.U66 8313 2009 C843'.54 C2009-903867-6

Cover design: Angel Guerra/Archetype
Interior text design: Tannice Goddard/Soul Oasis Networking
Printer: Friesens

CORMORANT BOOKS INC.
215 SPADINA AVENUE, STUDIO 230, TORONTO, ON CANADA M5T 2C7
www.cormorantbooks.com

CONTENTS

For Cécile

For Jean-Paul,
Louise,
Alain,
Nicole

There is definitely a connection between the journey and the body, and the sea we behold, we lose sight of, we tirelessly seek.

— SYLVIE MASSICOTTE

Au pays des mers

PRELUDE

STEP BY STEP

YOU SHOULD BEGIN. JUST WRITE one sentence. Others are sure to join it, and then others, followed by more sentences. You would eventually have a text. You aren't asking of yourself that you write a great text, but simply a text, one that holds together. Yet the computer screen remains empty. Empty and grey. It's not for lack of trying. Until now, you haven't been able to see yourself as a woman who could leave everything behind, who could go off to start a new life, board a ship hoisting an unknown flag, sail away to explore islands at the ends of the earth.

You may as well admit it — you don't belong to the race of adventuresses. Neither does your mother, nor your grandmother. Still, there was that woman among your ancestors who came and settled in New France at the age of sixteen with her second husband. She would have four husbands. Her son François accompanied Joliette on his expeditions. And her great-great-grandson Bruno went to New York to study at a time when few people studied.

Something has been lost in the family. You have all become sedentary, you don't know why. Fear perhaps, an old fear that rivets you to your lives. An ancient memory, the word *catastrophe*, tattooed onto your skin in large letters, causing your heart to beat wildly at night, in your dreams. When you wake up, faceless shadows linger on your bedroom walls. Lying very still, you patiently wait for them to fade. You have learned to cultivate patience as others do orchids.

It's pointless to keep trying — you won't be able to write this text. You decide to close the file so you can open another one, the file of your novel, where women appear who dare to start over. Anne, for example, a Martin, like your grandmother. Anne did decide to leave everything behind. Her work, her friends, her mother. It took a great deal of courage. Or humility. One morning she realized that even without her, the world would go on turning. She wasn't able to make other people happy, so why not make herself happy?

You aren't quite so humble. Or else your family is tactful enough to make you think they need you. You are happy, as happy as someone who isn't totally deluded can be. Perhaps that is why it has never occurred to you to walk away from it all. You like your life, even with the darkness you carry inside you, the darkness that would follow you even if you took refuge in the heart of some faraway desert. One can run away from one's parents, husband, children, country, one can leave one's heart behind, but not one's soul.

You travel, of course. You have visited crowded cities and picture-postcard landscapes, you have swum in the same sea as Ulysses, and like Proust you have admired Vermeer's *View of Delft*, but you always come back to your home base, this house whose walls you carefully painted yourself. This is where you write. In the morning you sit up in bed, with your dictionaries, and your small world fills up, you dream in the company of characters you would like to meet. Sometimes you have them do things you've never had the courage to do yourself and you are joyful until bedtime. As if you briefly opened a window on the woman you could have been in another life, someone you barely knew.

You won't say that fiction creates you — you'd feel as though you repeated the clichés one reads in rushed interviews. You couldn't stop writing, even if you were offered all possible lives. Writing actually takes up more and more space in your days. It is always with you, it fights the darkness that sometimes spreads through your whole body. You see yourself as a tightrope walker who is slowly, intently, crossing the ring on her wire, but there is no one there to cheer you on. You go forward alone.

But you *are* going forward, step by step. You continue on your way. You will live to a ripe old age without ever casting off your moorings, like the last women of your line. Is that so bad? Will you feel regret as your hand freezes forever on the keyboard of a computer? You don't think so, but who knows what will go through your mind then? You may suddenly be sorry you weren't one of those flamboyant women you admire, on rainy evenings, in television reports.

You often say one should strive to discover all the possibilities of one's writing. Doesn't the same hold true for one's life? You are ready to admit that now, even though you have difficulty writing it down. Already you turn around to look a long way back, and what you see is an unflattering image of yourself. Nevertheless, you will shape it into sentences, since you have no choice. You promised to write this text and you have always tried to keep your word. So you may as well begin.

I

A HAPPY BABEL

WE WOULDN'T BE BORED — ENDLESSLY, hopelessly bored, like the summer before. The corner restaurant, the dance hall on Saturday night after the workweek at the playground, always the same conversations. A few months back, the word *Expo* had entered our vocabulary. It fired our imaginations, like the documentaries about Africa shown at school — women with ebony skin, their dresses so flowery they looked indecent. Our own mothers went to Mass in suits adorned with a string of fake pearls. In our orderly world, we were more conscious of the Puritan roots of the Loyalists than of the Quiet Revolution. We listened to Adamo, the Beatles, Claude Léveillée, but didn't know how to say *free love* or *contraception*, let alone *abortion*.

It would be a summer of discoveries. We knew it. We sang *Un jour, un jour* and pictured ourselves already in Montréal. We would take the metro to the islands for the first time, we'd spend the day in exotic surroundings, eat strange food, meet people we never mixed with at home. We would become teenagers who have travelled, like the daughters of ambassadors, adventurers, millionaires. Or like those beautiful hostesses we saw on television. Barely older than us, they looked straight at the camera like women. We didn't know what that stemmed from: their designer outfits, the fact they spoke English, or some other knowledge, an intimate one, so intimate we didn't dare hint at it among ourselves. Suddenly the world was opening up. Or it had shattered, rather, like a china ornament, revealing other, unsuspected worlds. One could live differently, dress differently, love without fear, without regrets. Nothing would ever be the same again.

Expo was the bus chartered by the Playgrounds Association, a two-hour ride, the fun of travelling with friends, a whole day of pure delight, a spot even more beautiful than on photographs, long lines of cars, and patient waiting, since we weren't as lucky as Montréalers. They took the metro and away they went … twenty minutes later they stood in front of the French or British Pavilion. They could come during the week. Many had even bought a passport. One woman told us with a radiant smile that she came every Thursday.

I'd felt a twinge of longing. Some day I, too, would live in a big city. I would have money, I'd have the leisure to see all the shows I wanted. I would go on holiday to the most faraway countries, Thailand and Japan. *Education is the gateway to opportunity*, teachers kept telling us. All we needed to do was study: Latin, Greek, English and literature. Yes, literature promised us a never-ending Expo. So many writers had travelled! I would wind up in countries resembling those of the pavilions I visited almost religiously that summer. Like everyone else of my generation, I would be invincible. Life would bring me no unpleasant surprises. I would carry out my wildest plans. I would follow the example of those who had boldly created an island so they could build the eighth wonder of the world. Québec even had its own pavilion, as if it were a country …

That summer lingers in my memory as a time of unbridled enthusiasm, of rock-solid faith. On my way home from my town, I begin to smile as soon as the bus drives onto the Jacques-Cartier Bridge. As I crane my neck towards the dirty window, I attempt to revive old images. A sculpture, a painting, a dish sampled at the India Pavilion, the evenings at La Ronde with my pals. But nothing appears. Only hazy, fleeting impressions. The exhilaration I'd felt in the metro, which I would feel again on my first flight, a few years later. The sensation of freedom as I found myself in a crowd where nobody knew me, the thrill of belonging to a human community with billions of faces I wanted to be radiant. I cannot recall ever giving a thought to poverty, slavery, or suffering at Expo. Perhaps because I didn't wish to. What I saw was a clean, reassuring world, quite safe on islands protected by the lazily flowing St. Lawrence.

We, too, were protected, we felt. It never occurred to us we might run into crooks, or perverts. We talked to anyone who knew French. And we put into practice our English classes. *Where are you from? Is it your first trip in Canada?* Often, we exchanged addresses, a telephone number. *If you come to Germany, call me. Of course.* We now had friends from Los Angeles to Tokyo. When I got home, I locked their names away in a little box. I can't recall what I did with it — probably lost it during one of my many moves. I know I didn't throw it away because I would have remembered. After forty years one can't really be sure of anything, though.

I do have one totally sharp, vivid memory. Expo was drawing to an end. It was my great friend Luce's birthday and her parents had driven us to Montréal. We had mapped out a precise itinerary for ourselves. We wanted to visit all the pavilions we hadn't seen yet — never mind that the waits grew longer and longer as the season advanced. I can't remember at what pavilion we were lining up, but Luce and I had been waiting for at least two hours, while a hostess was doing her best to entertain us. She encouraged people of different nationalities to sing a song from their country. Most of them cheerfully complied. Then, perhaps at the end of her tether, she hit upon an idea: to ask those whose birthday it was to raise their hand. I pointed to my friend. Immediately a glorious cacophony rang out. It rose into the air, sent a thrill through Île Notre-Dame, swept us up in its joyfulness. The crowd sang "Happy Birthday" to Luce in every possible language.

Our eyes filled with tears. Luce and I were deeply moved. This was a happy Babel, a Babel at last reconciled. At peace. Man and his World. We would never forget it. Never, ever forget that blessed moment, September 11, 1967. From then on, September 11 would symbolize our highest hopes.

SNOW-COVERED EYES

HE HATED HER. HE HATED her the way a man might hate a woman he loves. That truth suddenly leaped out at her. Stark. Glaring. She would never be able to bring herself to repeat the words he had spoken. They made her vaguely ashamed, guilty for not going along with everything. Yes guilty, that was what she felt. How she had found the strength to tell him, as she looked him straight in the eye, that they'd better part, she didn't know. But already the vice was loosening. She would be able to remain in her chair opposite him until the end of the meal without making a fuss, as though she were someone else. They had only got as far as the first course.

It had started to snow. At the next table, people talked about the blizzard that was forecast. *At least twenty-five centimetres. What a country!* She had a sudden vision of the early settlers, their isolation on the concession roads buried beneath the snow. Did they sink into despair? she wondered. Now she, too, found herself in a strange city, which she would soon have to face. This was her own city, though, where she had walked and laughed and slept since the day she was born. The city where she met him and they made love for the first time.

In just a few minutes the window had turned white. One could hardly see the few passersby who had ventured out. With him, hand in hand, she had walked so often through the driving snow. Then, she had felt that nothing, not a single hurdle, blocked her way. *Will we see each other again?* he asked her quite humbly, and she replied she didn't know. She would need to relearn her jumbled body, to survive the destruction. *I love you. You love me. We love each other*. Lips searching for one another in brightly flowered sheets.

She barely noticed that the kidneys were tough. *Shall I tell the waiter to take them back?* he asked. She shook her head. She would only have a few bites anyway. He seemed to have grown fond of her again. Perhaps that was easier now, since there was nothing left to salvage between them. She pushed her plate away and waited. He hadn't finished yet. This was probably the last time she would see him lift his fork with that slight twisting of his hand. This detail shattered her. In a few months' time they'd meet in a restaurant like this one, they'd give each other a polite peck on the cheek, they wouldn't want to admit to themselves that their love now only existed in a distant memory. They'd exchange a few pleasantries before heading towards separate tables. During the meal, they'd barely throw each other an uneasy glance.

The restaurant had emptied out early. People must have felt the need to barricade themselves. A thick cover of snow swallowed the street. One forgot that beyond the window there was a city, a gasping, struggling, choking city. She had finished her coffee. She was silent. She could still see the hard look in his eyes as his words dealt her the final blow. The waiter brought the bill. She needed to tear herself away from that table. She insisted on paying her share — she wasn't going to let him take care of it, not this night. She asked him to let her leave first so they wouldn't have to say goodbye to each other in the wilderness outside. She wrapped herself up warmly and headed towards the door.

Now the city had come to a complete standstill. But she would walk — yes, walk — to put off the moment when she'd find herself at home alone. She would go forward by placing one foot in front of the other, carefully, like people who had to go forward without knowing where they were going. She pictured François Paradis in the snowstorm, blinded, all that love he felt for Maria Chapdelaine.

She pushed up her coat sleeve to look at her watch. Almost ten o'clock. He should be back at his place by now. He was getting ready to watch the news. He was saved. She had no idea where she was. Her snow-covered eyes could no longer make out the street names. Perhaps she had begun to lose her way.

THE BAR

CLINKING OF CHEAP GLASSES THROUGH bland music, punctured by laughter, and those words that suddenly rose in waves and died out in my ears, *How nice! Exactly!* All those strangers trying to make a life for themselves at the border of their lives. But was I so different from them? What was I doing in this out-of-the-way place when I never set foot in a bar in Montréal? What possessed me to come and lecture at the ends of the earth! It had to be fatigue, the tight schedule of the day, jet lag. I had woken up at dawn that morning. I might as well accept it — I would never be one of those writers who could live out of a suitcase. One needed to come out of one's shell, though, give up one's little routine, so I said yes, I accepted, as though making a flashy gesture, and forced myself for a few days to become a woman who could savour the tang of the ocean air on some faraway shore, who could order her meals in another language, who could say the right thing on every occasion.

I always felt out of place in a bar, caught between the din and the bad light. Why wasn't there a single bar in the world with decent lighting? I had never seen a single properly lit classroom either, and yet in a classroom I was able to talk, breathe, and listen, I could laugh freely without having the impression I was a character in a play. To keep the woman who brought me here company, I ordered *A light beer, please*, which suited me best before I went to sleep — soon I'd be in the tub, it wouldn't be long now. I smiled at Olga. Her name was Olga. Yes, she was delightful. Twenty-five years ago, she travelled halfway across the planet to settle in this very spot. That's what fascinated me, people who left everything behind and tried to recreate a family of sorts in the place they adopted as their home. I had always lived a hundred and fifty kilometres from the hospital where my mother gave birth to me one sweltering afternoon. In a place where the winters were bitterly cold, so cold it frightened the people here. Here, it was summer all year round. Perhaps Olga preferred such a climate to the winters of my country, but it might also have been one of those random events we call fate, which sometimes works out for the best.

Olga had met a man here. They had a house together, a garden, a bank account, grown-up children, who were thinking of leaving, too. That was her only heartache: she wouldn't have the pleasure of seeing her grandchildren grow up. She had a cheerful nature, though, and her eyes soon brightened again. She asked me if I had children. I opened my mouth to answer, but a handsome young man appeared and Olga got up at once, held out her hand to him, pointed to the empty chair beside me. He gracefully shook his head, gestured towards a group of friends sitting at the back of the room. Then he said goodbye to us and, just as gracefully, went to join them.

Jeremy, the son of a friend of mine, Olga whispered with a faraway look in her eyes. *A dear friend who is dying of cancer*, she added, clearing her throat.

Oddly enough, the voices in the bar had all but evaporated, as if Olga had been overheard. I glanced sideways at Jeremy, at the far end, deep in conversation with a girl — all I saw of her was her thick blond hair. I wondered if she was pretty, if he was trying to pick her up. I wondered how anyone whose mother was dying could possibly be on the prowl. But I dismissed the thought straight away. Was I the guardian of morals? Didn't life go on even when people disappeared around us? Not a week went by, in fact, that I didn't hear of someone I knew having cancer, even children. The word *cancer* was all you heard these days. A few years ago, it didn't crop up in conversations quite as often.

Across from me, Olga still stared at the same spot, in silence. What images filed past her eyes, I wondered. I took a sip of beer to draw her attention. I needed to ask her a question, get her to talk about her friend. I wanted to know everything about her illness. Nosiness, voyeurism, an innate morbidity? I couldn't pinpoint the real reasons. Perhaps I simply wanted to exorcise my fear, so that back in my room I could tell myself in front of the peaceful landscape on the wall that I would ship out at ninety-nine, and not a day sooner. Even before I could think of the right question, Olga began to speak, still with that faraway look in her eyes, as if she were commenting off-camera on a movie she projected inside her head. She'd met Helen when she arrived here — a pretty, cheerful, determined woman who was completing her doctorate. A thesis defence that had become famous in the department's history. An old fossil made a ridiculous remark to the girl. She exploded into a fit of laughter that set off the audience. The whole room began to laugh. The old fossil left, outraged. They'd had to apologize to him, bring him back into the room, pretend they agreed with his twaddle. Olga laughed heartily and so did I. I pictured certain faces, certain researchers who thought they were God. How tempting it would be to teach them a little lesson.

Understandably, Helen didn't want to teach. She had found a job in the civil service, got married, divorced, then met the man she lived with, the father of Jeremy who was just opening his wallet to pay for his second draft beer. What did he know about his mother? A young man didn't ask himself such questions. He wanted friends, a girl in his bed. He was getting an education, looked towards the future. Ten or twenty years from now, queries would arise in his mind, but all that would be left would be a name carved in a headstone. What child could boast that they knew everything about their mother? Didn't we always make up a life for her? But I thought like a novelist. People were deeply enamoured of the truth, especially when it involved their roots. It was all very well to wrestle with fiction, tamper with the facts page after page to make them plausible, we believed without reservation whatever our mother told us. Not just our mother, but our friends, our acquaintances, and Olga, too, who was now boldly sketching Helen's past for me. And I wanted to believe her. I needed to grasp a truth, the truth, like those medals we wore around our necks to protect us, when we were children.

Helen was the epitome of the perfect woman. She had never drawn a single puff from a cigarette and had a glass of wine only at Christmas or at weddings. She converted to whole-wheat bread long before it was fashionable. She ate fruit, vegetables, fish, never any sweets, headed for the swimming pool twice a week, played tennis, went in for mountain hiking. And always kept her spirits up, even when her little girl drowned in the swimming pool. She didn't break down but went back to work two weeks after the funeral. Life must go on, she would say. Olga started to laugh, not maliciously, just to relieve the tension, and because of the rapport between us, because she wanted to share her fondness of Helen with a stranger who was going to leave in a couple of days and wouldn't repeat what she had heard in this bar.

Now I was wide awake. I said *Yes* to the waiter who asked me if I'd have another beer, and Olga ordered another Scotch. Tomorrow, we'd have drooping eyelids, but never mind, we'd been sleep deprived before. Our talk had become intimate, we had begun to share secrets. Our first names rang out in the conversation. I sensed Olga relaxing a little more with each sentence. It was such a comfort to be able to share this sorrow, she admitted, the sorrow of seeing Helen deteriorating, of knowing that in a few short weeks she wouldn't be there anymore. But not just that heartache — another one as well, a worse one, that of seeing how Helen had truly come into her own in the last little while. Olga stopped abruptly. I must have thrown her an odd look. Did I hear that right? Yes, she continued, weighing her words, Helen had changed — for the better, she stressed. She was claiming a space for herself, which she had never done. She stood up for what she believed in, stated her preferences, actually started eating fast food during her chemo. Olga smiled. The day before, Helen ordered a pizza — she who would never make one, not even when her son asked her to on his birthday.

Olga's smile ebbed away. I spotted a discreet tear at the corner of her eye. I looked away and focused on a well-known painting on the wall, a reproduction of a scene by an artist whose name I couldn't remember. My memory was playing tricks on me again. *With the passing years, we fall apart*, my doctor often said with his usual cynicism. Fortunately, I was in good health, but no one could predict the future. Would I change if I found out I was going to die soon? *Why allow yourself to live when you are about to die?* Olga murmured, as if she had heard my question. We dropped the subject, even though it would have been so easy to go into all those theories on how the emotions affected the body. So easy, also, to open up to Olga — about that friend, for example, who had confided to me a few weeks before she died that, in order to get better, she would have had to change too many things in her life. As if dying brought her relief! I'd had terrible dreams that night and had woken up with an indefinable feeling — dread, compassion, despair. How could a woman in the prime of life let herself slip away like that? And would I, if I discovered some day that I needed to change my life, be able to do it — I mean, still be able to do it after so many endings and new beginnings? I thought of that man, in his late fifties, who didn't have the courage to leave his native Europe to follow my sister Edith, whom he had fallen madly in love with. I had thought him spineless at the time, but perhaps I needed to come here, to this out-of-the-way bar, to fully weigh my words.

I tell you things I don't admit to my friends or relatives, I said to Olga, amused. We laughed openly. It felt good! I looked at my watch. I wouldn't be at my best in the morning, but what did I know? I might give a very good lecture. *We must live*, Olga declared as she got up. *Not wait till we're at death's door*. That was obviously not lost on Jeremy, who was ordering another beer. Olga said goodbye to him before she pushed open the heavy wooden door. Off in the distance, the waves crashed on the rocks with a sound like splintering glass. But even when it was brittle, it was still the sea, which soothed. I thought I could make a fresh start here. I told Olga, but she didn't reply. And I didn't expect her to. She knew I was just trying to calm my fears.

THE THIMBLE

THERE IT IS, UP ON the shelf, right in front of your eyes. You point at it. The shopkeeper slides the glass away and drops the thimble into your hands. It's heavy, made of solid silver, finely chiselled, with a tiny blue stone you don't know the name of. You simply must have this magnificent thimble, and you are capable of bargaining. As in the *souk* in Tunis, where you picked up that *djellaba* you love so much.

Do you have a collection? asks an Englishman you barely know. Absently you reply, *No, but my mother does*. That is all you say, your mind already on the transaction. You don't tell him it's you who assembled that thimble collection as you happened to come across them on your trips. First the rather plain china one you bought for her in Paris, then a second one in Washington, then others in Venice, Seattle, Athens, and where else? Oh yes, Brussels, then Puerto Vallarta, and your daughter has started bringing back thimbles for her grandmother, too. Your mother now has two dozen pieces. She puts them where everyone can see them — on the bottom shelf of her cabinet with the glass doors, in front of the fancy cups and antique curios.

But you've never spotted one like this before, with the lovely, baroque richness of the eastern jewellery you've been seeing on women in Marrakech's well-to-do neighbourhoods. Your mother has worn more thimbles than rings on her fingers, dressmaker's thimbles, made of cheap metal, but useful when she sewed winter coats for you out of old coats given to her by your aunts. First, she had to take the garment apart, then wash and stretch the woollen fabric. On October nights, in the yellow lamplight, she would study the pattern and try to puzzle out how to fit it onto the material. Yes, *study* was the word she used: she set an example for you on all those fall evenings when you saw her bending over the table, scissors in hand.

Marrakech. That name, when you were a child, conjured up a world of stories, with lamps harbouring genies, and thieves held captive behind heavy rocks that would only move if one knew the formula. You never thought there were women who sewed in Marrakech, never thought you would ever bargain here for a silver thimble. You never thought that some day you would find yourself at the gates of the desert, home of the nomads, who don't grow attached to the places where they settle, who learn very early to leave landscapes and towns behind. Never thought that with each trip you would move a little farther away from the woman you still call Mama.

She would have loved to see Paris, of course. The Eiffel Tower, the Champs-Élysées, Notre Dame. She looked at these for a long time in brochures you gave her. Sometimes, when you visit her, she fantasizes out loud: she is still young, she strolls along the quays of the Seine. There is the Louvre and, further down, the Jardin des Tuileries. She stops at a sidewalk café, has a glass of red wine. Behind these tiny episodes that make up a trip, you hear all those things she doesn't dare say — she belongs to the group of people who take holidays, she is a cherished woman.

A few years ago, you wanted to take her to Paris, but she refused. She had reached the age when dreams no longer set their sights on reality. You insisted, just to be polite, but you could tell she had made up her mind, and perhaps, deep down, in spite of your bouts of nostalgia, you would rather go on travelling without her. Who knows, after all, what you really want.

A hundred and fifty dirhams? That's too much. You say this with bold self-confidence, as if your honour were at stake. But you have learnt that a merchant expects you to bargain, so you wait for his reaction. *How much do you want to pay?* You come up with a figure, *Ninety dirhams*, and he suggests a hundred and forty. The two of you will settle on a hundred and ten or a hundred and twenty dirhams. You will because he wants to sell and you want to buy. You must have that thimble.

It's yours. All yours. On the way back to the hotel, you skip along as when you were a little girl bringing home your report card and you were top of the class. Mama would smile as she looked over the pale yellow booklet. She deserved your high marks, as she does this beautiful thimble, with the tiny blue drop that probably isn't a precious stone.

You say hello to the doorman as you walk into your hotel, a man who cannot be earning much money, and the mere thought brings back the ghosts from your past — your father's badly paid job, the money problems, the bleakness of those grey years. While you climb the stairs, the silver thimble doesn't feel as heavy anymore at the bottom of your handbag, and the mother from your childhood is now just another woman in the sea of humanity that tries every day to defy poverty, a poverty that cannot be called destitution.

You put the thimble down on the glass table near the bed. As it sits there on its own, away from the store, it looks bare, forlorn, incapable of magic feats. You sit down. You feel like a fool. Why did you buy that insignificant thing? You'll take it home in your luggage nonetheless. You will give it to your mother. You'll tell her about your trip. That is all she wants nowadays. And you cannot erase the life she has lived, you have given up on storybook wizardry.

You will bring her this trinket to make her forgive you.

BLUE

I TURNED OFF THE ENGINE of the car and got out with my basket of blueberries. The curtains of the house were still drawn. Not a sound. Dead calm. The radio wasn't playing its usual pop tunes. I knocked. I knocked harder. No answer. Where on earth could Madame Robitaille be? Surely not very far. At a neighbour's place or the hairdresser's. You can't go very far in this village.

I had already gone down the stairs again when I heard a hoarse cry. I turned around. A woman of indeterminate age motioned to me and, with a pounding heart, I went back up the steps. I found Madame Robitaille slumped in a flower-patterned armchair, wearing a housecoat with a different flower pattern. I must have turned pale, because the woman tried to reassure me straight away: Madame Robitaille was fine, yes, she was fine. Only, she had just had a shock. That very morning, Virginie had been found lifeless in her apartment. A sordid murder. Who? How? Why? All these questions rushed into my mind, but the words wouldn't cross my lips. I took refuge in the other flowery armchair.

When I had arrived the previous Saturday with a basket of raspberries, Virginie was sitting in the kitchen. Dark-haired, around thirty, she was an accountant who worked for a large company in the nearest town, she told me. A young woman like thousands of others. She was in the village for her father's birthday and took advantage of the opportunity to go and say hello to her old babysitter. I wanted to slip away quickly, but Madame Robitaille had made me stay. Wasn't I a friend of her son's, the woman who had rented the old family home on the fifth concession for the summer? I would have preferred the word *collaborator*, but didn't want to contradict her. Besides, the word *friend* covered a wide enough range to be suited to any occasion. This was not the time to give voice to my scruples as a translator, so I agreed. Yes, I was a friend of Louis's, and the elderly woman smiled, as if her son had briefly left his publishing house to drop in for a visit himself.

There was no need for me to make conversation. Virginie talked about her life, her plans, her holidays, that new boyfriend she'd met thanks to a website. Taken aback, Madame Robitaille had asked one question after another — she who had met her late husband, Gérard, at a neighbour's house. In sixty years, everything had changed, including love: numerous lovers, contraception, divorces. What was going to happen to relationships over the next two generations? Virginie had replied to her in a subtle, intelligent way. I liked her, I really did. I had had a cup of tea with her, delighted in getting to know her, even though I normally did not leave my computer for very long.

Madame Robitaille began to cry, and the woman — Mathilde, as I found out — tried to calm her down. I finally learned certain facts. That very morning, Virginie had been found underneath her mattress. She had been there for a few days, but, to find out more, we would have to wait for the inquest, the autopsy, the fingerprints, all those things one sees on television in B movies. No suspect behind bars yet. *What a ridiculous idea, choosing a boyfriend through the Internet!* Madame Robitaille blurted out, and I felt ashamed because the idea had occurred to me, too, but I had rejected it instantly. I was definitely getting old: I was forgetting that, when I was young, girls took boys whom they had met in bars into their beds without even knowing their first name, and none of them had been murdered. Virginie's murderer could be a travelling salesman, a burglar, a former lover, a neighbour, the landlord. Don't they say that most of the time women know their attackers?

This was not the right moment to argue with Madame Robitaille, however. I tried instead to persuade her to come and spend the rest of the day with us, in her childhood home. She must have been reluctant to be flooded with old memories. She would rather stay in the village, she would go to Mathilde's house. Mathilde was her cousin, and also Virginie's aunt by marriage. I left, feeling relieved, but also anxious to be alone on the road.

As I arrived home, I didn't ask myself why Mark had run outside as soon as he'd heard wheels crunching the gravel.

He was worried — hadn't I noticed how late it was? I could have called him. Wasn't that precisely what the cellphone was for: to let him know when I was going to be late? Strangely enough, his anger reassured me. Someone cared about me. Someone loved me in this increasingly violent world. Mark would send people looking for me if I disappeared. I finally broke down and began to sob.

I was unable to translate a single worthwhile paragraph that afternoon. The words remained locked inside themselves. The nouns failed to form connections with the verbs. The sentences had no rhythm. Terrified, they watched me, and then faded away before Virginie's death mask. I got up. I went out to rock myself back and forth on the white veranda that runs around the house, soothed by the creaking of the wood. I closed my eyes and listened to the rustling of the trees while trying to name them, as if to anchor myself in reality. Everything was fine, just fine. But all it would take was some deranged man following me and placing a knife at my throat as I turned the key in the lock … It had happened to a friend recently. She had escaped unharmed with admirable coolness of mind, but can one blame all the women who don't share her instinct for survival? Probably Virginie never had a chance to speak, or scream, or fight.

I started to shake. Was it wise, I wondered, to stay here, at the very end of this country road, in the middle of nowhere? The previous week, Mark had gone to meet the author he was translating. I had spent the night alone without being the slightest bit afraid. But if Mark had to go to Montréal again, I would definitely go with him. Actually, when Mark got back, he had suggested we reserve the house for the following summer — it was scorching hot in the city, and, with global warming, the dog days were going to get worse every year. I had agreed, but now I wasn't so sure anymore.

Mark came to join me on the veranda. He wasn't able to work either. The grey cat we had been feeding since the beginning of the holidays rubbed against my leg, then jumped on me, and I felt calmed. Thanks to this nameless stray, I could still believe a little in the gentleness of the world. I forgot the question that had been bothering me since childhood — the question of evil. I had never asked myself who we were, where we came from, or where we were going. I was a woman, I came out of the womb of another woman who would return to the earth some day, and I would simply follow her there. That is what I once replied in a philosophy course at university, much to the contempt of my fellow students. But with regard to evil, I had no answer. Two hands squeezing a woman's neck until she could no longer breathe, a cruel act like that — I didn't understand. Anyway, no matter how many books I'd read, I had never been able to comprehend the maze of the human soul. And, as the years went by, incidents such as this affected me more and more. How fragile would I be at Madame Robitaille's age?

I suggested we take the cat home with us in September. We couldn't abandon it. It would get used to the polluted city air, just as we had. I promised I would look after it, and Mark smiled. Obviously, he had already adopted the cat. He proposed we call it Blue, since it had appeared out of the blue. I wondered all of a sudden if Virginie had a cat, too, and tears streamed down my cheeks again. It was all very well for me to try and save a cat, but that didn't do anything to end the infinite misery in the world.

Blue began to purr. My spirits picked up a little. I should get moving, look after myself and others. Doesn't each day come with its share of hopelessness? I put Blue down and got up. I was an upright human being again, capable of tackling the evening routine: prepare the vinaigrette, wash the lettuce, toss it, lay the tablecloth, set the table, chew, tidy up the kitchen with Mark, get washed, wait till sleep overtook me.

When I woke up, my head felt as awful as if I had drunk a bottle of cognac. But a garland of sounds wound itself around my ear. Then it broke off for two bars, to start again at once, as if marked by a stopwatch. Birdsong — the new day was trying to find a foothold. I clung to Mark, his spicy smell. That morning, I would go to the village to see how Madame Robitaille was getting along. She might have information about Virginie's death. I would also reserve the house for next summer. The elderly lady would only be too pleased, as would her son.

I heard Blue. He was scratching at the door. He had spent the night in the fields, he was hungry. I got up. I had to go and feed him.

THE STAR

WITH NICOTINE-STAINED FINGERTIPS SHE stubbed out her cigarette in an art-glass ashtray. I tried not to pay attention to her fake-gypsy getup in order to suppress an unbearable wave of uneasiness. How had I ended up here, in front of this fortune teller who, Dominique had promised, would tell me all about my future? Distress. There are periods that are darkened by distress, and one longs for reassurance — you'll find happiness again, summer will return. There are times when our gullibility knows no bounds.

I see a better life for you. I almost replied, *It would be difficult to imagine worse*, but checked myself. I had come, I ought to play the game. All I said, a bit too flippantly, was *La dolce vita*. The woman's face lit up. She lowered her eyes and began to speak in a sonorous, musical language, in which I recognized the expression *dolce, dolce vita*. To remind her I was still there, I asked, *Do you believe life can be sweet?* Taken aback, she turned her head towards me, stared at me, looking sad. *For you, yes*. I insisted, *And for you?* She picked up the cards and murmured, *In my life, there is no room for the future*. The veins in her hands seemed as hard as rope. I had only just noticed and couldn't take my eyes off them while she shuffled the cards.

How old was this woman? Probably in her sixties, her late sixties. Would I still feel I had a future at that age?

The late-afternoon light spilled over the table, after passing through a jumble of plants and knick-knacks. Strangely enough, I felt better and better with this woman, who had laid out the tarot cards on the table and started predicting the most ludicrous blessings for me. To show her I wasn't taken in, I pointed to the Tower and said, *Dolce vita?* She stopped talking, aware I didn't believe her. For a few minutes, she remained silent and aloof. I felt like a little girl who'd been caught out. She was trying to earn her living as well as she could. Should she go and work as a cleaning lady at her age? She'd had enough of me and with good reason. I knew I'd been insufferable lately. I was about to get up to leave when she said, *The hard times are behind you. Your life is ruled by the Star, you see, but you don't trust me.*

I suddenly felt like screaming. How could she expect me to believe her, with all the bad news, the illnesses, depressions, and breakups piling up around me, and that friend who had just tried to kill herself — a world we hadn't known existed in our teenage years, *The order of the catastrophe*, I had said to Dominique one evening when we'd had one drink too many. I rubbed a tear from my cheek. As if she hadn't noticed, the woman went on, *Much peace of mind, much love.*

Getting angrier and angrier, I told her to stop. Visibly annoyed, too, she asked, *Why did you come, then?* Yes, why did I? What was I doing here? I got out my wallet, apologizing, but she put her gnarled hand on mine. *No. If you don't believe me, don't pay me*. Then she invited me to have a cup of tea with her.

The maple leaves almost reached us on the balcony. In a few days it would be June, at last. The air was turning balmy. The spring had been so harsh, we had given up waiting for the warm weather, but now the city began to breathe again. It was coming to life, rustling, whispering. I quietly sipped my tea. Slowly, I relaxed with this woman, a stranger and yet so familiar. Without looking at her, I said, *I insist on paying you. For the sake of hope*.

A VACANT WORLD

THIS IS THE PLACE WHERE the sea gives up, tired of dragging itself over the pebbles. For several hours, it advances, threatens to engulf you, and then stops, seems to hesitate, and slowly recedes with its grey, murmuring waves, regular as clockwork. The mechanism never breaks down, no one gives it a thought. At the hotel, the daily routine is always the same. Getting up, breakfast, and the beach, then lunch, more sun, and dinner in the dining room with the pink tablecloths, refined dishes. The envied holiday life of characters in movies. Now and then a polite conversation, by the piano, with someone you are indifferent to. Afterwards, you'll only enjoy the silence more.

All that will remain of your stay will be a golden tan and a few baubles you will have bought so you won't come home empty-handed. You always return to this spot, and ask for room 314, with this balcony overlooking the sea. To listen to the surf as you would to a concert for days on end is all you want to do. This year, however, you haven't fallen under the spell. The sea is useless, a scrap-iron grey that leaves you unmoved. You can't understand it: you have travelled thousands of kilometres to be faced with your own insensitivity. Around you, a vacant world. Perhaps you should make up your mind to rent a jeep, and, with a guide, follow the road southward and head inland, towards Timbuktu. The desert perhaps. But you do nothing of the sort. You content yourself with picking up a book. You content yourself with dreaming.

In the distance, fishermen make their way towards the harbour in their shabby little boats. Yesterday, you saw them up close, during a sightseeing trip. Their craft moored in the harbour, men and boys were repairing nets and waited for evening to put out to sea again. They make up two shifts, the guide explained, one working days and the other nights. For the first time, the sea looked like a huge factory to you, where workers clock in before disappearing inside. You have seen your father leaving for work. He would come back in the morning, and your mother would ask you to be quiet and allow him to sleep.

The place where you come from has mountains, and lakes large enough to get lost on, but no sea. The sea is for the people who live on the coast, who don't seem to be from the same country as you, people with furrowed faces. Sometimes you hear them on television, with their singsong accents. They, too, talk about fishing, and you listen closely, as you did to those uncles who came to visit your parents in the wintertime, when you were a child, when the harvest was finally in the barns. You were polite, a polite little girl, just present enough to nod or shake your head when the conversation required it. You were a child of the city, with its noisy streets, ear-splitting car horns, the boys from school you managed to bump into at the movies. Some day, you would know love. Some day, you would exchange your city for another one.

When did you first feel the urge to travel? You don't remember. It just happened. He had rented a car to go to the ends of the earth, and, being in love, you went with him. You discovered the endless stream of villages along the roads. Customs, vegetation becoming more exuberant day by day. You discovered the sea. That is where he told you he loved you. He went out that night, on some pretext or other, and didn't return. The next morning, you notified the police in your broken English and waited. They persuaded you to continue your trip. Sooner or later, you would have to set off again.

Near New York, you learned that the sea had spat out the body. What else did they tell you? It's a blank. The words hit a wall in your head. All you remembered, when you left the police station, was a single image, that of your lover, on the beach, his skin eaten into, rotten already. You got back behind the wheel and drove all night, listening to the blues, until the car stopped in front of your door. You called the rental company to come and pick it up. You have never driven since.

Here, it's still the Atlantic, but you watch it from another continent, as though that might help you to understand what will always be beyond your understanding. You have banished the word *suicide* from your vocabulary. Instead, you say warily, *he passed away*, when you happen to mention him. You never explain. You tell a new lover about your first trip, with Bernard, a friend. Then you change the subject — political scandals, trivial details from your childhood. Isn't childhood an inexhaustible source of tenderness when the present alone doesn't carry enough weight?

Of course, there have been other men. You have visited legendary islands, where heroes, bewitched by enchantresses, basked in their love for decades. You have known the waters where the sirens lived. You have dreamed of Asia from the shores of Crete, before discovering this devastated city you now return to every year. To the same hotel, room 314. You stay here for two weeks, watching the tide coming in and going out, as if it moved within your veins. Then you are on your way.

Again this year, you came alone. A challenge? The wish to face yourself? You don't know. Your new lover let you leave with the promise that, afterwards, you'd take a holiday together. You would go and join him in Casablanca. You would travel through the country in a northeasterly direction, until you reached the other sea. You agreed. You agree with everything he suggests — as if the fact of saying no put you in danger.

It happened with the death of your brother, Bernard, the eldest. One morning, the telephone woke you up. Another wrong number, you thought to yourself, annoyed, but straight away you recognized the voice of your sister. Then you heard your mother crying, blaming herself, and you mechanically took in the words they flung at you. *Ambulance*, *death certificate*, *funeral*. You'd be there in a few hours, you just needed to gather up your things. You would take the two o'clock train. Clothes, books, pencils, childhood photos — you piled it all into your suitcase, along with the card your brother sent you for your last birthday, as if you needed concrete proof of his existence.

No journey had ever seemed so short. You didn't read, though. You didn't chat with the man who sat next to you. You fastened on to the scenery, you let yourself be borne by the strangeness of the settings slipping past before your eyes: a tree too green for the season, a luxury inn painted a garish pink. The familiar places had turned into a heap of ghastly things you had never noticed. Nothing abolishes space the way ugliness does, since it disrupts continuity. All it takes is a nose too long for a face, an outside staircase that doesn't go with a house's facade, a cow with unattractive markings in a field, and the image is shattered. All that remains is the offending detail. You would think of that later, on your balcony, in front of the sea. Only the sea cannot be ugly — it can never be contained within a frame. Only the sea, shifting, changing, grandiose in spite of the wretchedness of its small boats.

That time, you didn't have to wait. You discovered the truth at once. Your brother had been found in the hall closet, tied to a beam. This is when the long litany of theories began: an unhappy love affair, a secret illness, financial problems, a nervous breakdown. Your mother filled the hours, and you agreed with her, to stave off an intolerable silence. You didn't try to understand. He wasn't your son, after all.

That night, you dreamt your brother smiled down at you from his heaven and came towards you, opening his arms like a lover. Yet your elder brother's suicide had nothing in common with the other Bernard's. It touched you in the oldest fibres of your being. The smothered laughter in the morning when you woke up before your parents, the quarrels around the table after a day at the playground, the pleasure of listening to Mama reading a bedtime story to help you fall asleep. Your brother had taken your childhood with him. Ahead lay the present without the past, the huge hole of the present that now needed to be filled, day after day.

You were perfect at the funeral. Then you went back to work and continued to listen to your mother: what could she have done to prevent what no one could foresee? You sat there, still without answers. You had joined the vast group of people who don't seek motives for actions, the crowd of unbelievers. Even without believing, one survives. All the same, there is desire. It will catch you off guard, as you turn around to admire a bookshop's window, or at the museum before a painting you would have liked to paint. You agree to go for a coffee, why not, and wind up at the movies, beside a man. What does it matter that he is called Bernard! You can't very well ask him to change his name.

As it happens, he just phoned. His playful voice covered the breaking of the waves while he murmured words of love to you, and suddenly the bed filled the entire room. You wondered why you had been so eager to bring your loneliness here. You immersed yourself in a travel guide and, on your balcony, flipped through long pages with names of cities in bold letters. Rabat, Meknès, Marrakech, with its fortune tellers and snake charmers. Why had you never gone to Marrakech? A voice, Bernard's, and the world had spun around, bringing back the memory of all living places. This was called *consolation*, perhaps. In the end, the tide would go out again, as it always had.

Tonight, no doubt, you will dream of ships crushed by the tentacles of a monster. You will kick and struggle, unable to cry out. You will open your eyes, your skin covered with sweat, and you will forget what kind of woman you were a few hours before, in the last rays of the sun. Once again, you'll go in search of water for your parched lips. You'll seek out the sound of the sea so you can confront your fear. At night, there is no redemption. Just this presence you cannot define, except sometimes in images. Just this thing that takes up all the space in your chest. Just your body collapsing in on itself until you no longer exist. But is that enough to keep you from exploring countries whose languages resonate in your ears like the echo of unknown music?

The staff at reception will be worried. You will kindly answer their questions. No, no one in your family is ill. You like the hotel very much. The room is just as nice as in previous years. The food is excellent, really. So why are you leaving before the end of your stay? They'll insist. To be done with it, you'll quietly tell them about that friend meeting you in Casablanca. Smiles will reappear on their faces. You'll become a woman like the others, who gets married and gives birth to children. They will carry your luggage to the taxi and wish you all the happiness in the world. They will want you to come and stay again next summer, with your fiancé. You will thank them, you'll promise. But you know you won't be back.

DOLL STORY

HE WAS LOOKING AT HER as if she were still a little girl. There was something childlike in her gestures, he told her a moment ago, when she laid her hand flat on the glass to stop him from pouring her more wine. Already woozy. He shouldn't get the impression that all it took was one or two drinks to … to what exactly? How could she be sure of the intentions of this man who had been chatting pleasantly with her for the past few minutes? She had been anticipating the big seduction scene. She knew he was attracted to her — he said so in front of her to a colleague, very clearly, so she would hear. She remembered lowering her eyes. Some men so readily voiced their desire, it threw her off balance at times. In that area, too, she was like a child.

It had taken nearly two years for them to meet again, here, at this restaurant in Chinatown, a delightful little place, he'd assured her. He had introduced the manager, a woman who spoke French amazingly well. They exchanged a few words. The ground had no longer given way under her feet. They could have a leisurely meal together, and talk, without her having to protect herself. Actually, the man was speaking about his plans: perhaps they could collaborate, undertake some interdisciplinary project. He uttered the word with pursed lips, to make her smile. They could collaborate, why not? It was a way of seeing each other again, of prolonging the moment.

She accepted another glass of wine. She was even the one who said with a laugh, *You may have to drive me home*. She was surprised at her own remark. How would it be interpreted? But she felt safe. This man wasn't the type to come on strong, or shower a woman with the usual compliments while having a meal with her. He only slipped *You are beautiful* into an ordinary sentence, a minute ago, like a statement of fact resulting from cold observation. He could just as well have asked whose auburn hair she had inherited. Yes, she felt safe. Her reserve had melted away. Here she was reminiscing.

Why did she open up to him so quickly? She barely knew him. Why him exactly, in this place that didn't lend itself at all to exchanging confidences, with those shouts and clattering plates? She talked and he seemed be listening. Was he really interested in that little broken-doll story? She would have sworn he was. Suddenly the incident became more important. She kept talking while making the most of her dramatic effects, like someone who might be accustomed to fiction. He was laughing. The event had gained substance, it existed between them. She laughed along with him. He placed his large hand on hers, pleased to see her looking happy, he explained. What struck him the first time he caught sight of her was her sadness.

What should she tell this man? He was waiting for an answer — he looked deeply into her eyes. She stammered something as she pulled her hand away. She turned her gaze towards the back of the restaurant, fixed some faraway spot, remembered the man who had come up to her on the platform of the metro and said, *There is such sadness in your face.* Dumbfounded, unable to move, she had simply said, *I'm fine, thanks.* Some visionary, no doubt. She might have known: his eyes had the blissful glow of the newly converted. She'd had to pull herself together to turn on her heel and walk away.

How could she escape? She could get up, take her bag, thank her table companion for the pleasant meal, and quietly leave. Yet she knew she wouldn't. She would disguise her confusion, pick up the conversation where they left off, at her father's reaction — who'd ever heard of a girl breaking her doll to find out how the eyes closed! She wouldn't get any more toys, not from him in any case. But the spell was broken. No one was interested in her childhood, after all. Traces, like everyone else's, lingering traces that chafed without causing real pain. Other women carried deep wounds. One only needed to open one's eyes. She had nothing to tell. What did she expect from this meal? Why had she agreed to come?

There was a tear on her cheek and he apologized: he had been tactless, perhaps. She shook her head, no, let's just drop it. But he insisted. How could he get her to understand that he wasn't indifferent to her? This man was a tough one — she needed to play for time, to do something, preserve her image. Young woman in full possession of her faculties had lunch with distinguished man. They could have talked about the looming recession or the housing crisis. They could have flirted a bit, nothing too serious, just to prove to themselves they were still attractive. They would have kissed on their way out of the restaurant. We'll call each other, of course. Of course.

Do you feel the need to psychoanalyze all the women you take out for lunch? She just couldn't hold the bottled-up anger in check anymore. She took a sip of water. The meal was already spoiled anyway, the friendship too, plans for collaboration dropped. She only had to be patient for a few more minutes. The waitress was already bringing the desserts. He broke the silence, *Nothing is easy with you*. She snapped back, *I never said I was easy*, but regretted the bad pun. Why introduce sexuality when they were miles away from it? Something reassuring, probably, in her knowledge of men, a subtle bond that culminated in shared pleasure. But she felt helpless with him as he peered into her eyes to extract their secrets.

The eyes of a broken doll, he said, while she looked down, no longer able to bear his gaze. All the words had been spoken. They were ready to leave. She shouldn't have told him that doll story. She threw on her coat. She would have to try and get a grip on herself. She accepted a ride home. The weather had changed for the worse, he added quickly, as if he suspected she might change her mind. But she smiled. Above all, she must avoid giving an impression of fragility.

Caught in the rain, people were running across the street. Her eyes fixed on a little girl who clutched an old, soaking-wet doll. He saw it, too. Right then, she was sure of it, he took her by the arm, *Will we see each other again?* She shook her head, but he didn't appear to notice. He whispered in her ear, *You have nothing to fear from me.*

He shut the car door after her, got behind the wheel. The rain seemed to be easing off. She pointed it out to him. He agreed. He drove slowly, as if he didn't want to part from her. They were almost there. There they were. Now she should say goodbye to him, open the door, get out, but she couldn't bring herself to do it. Why not? She didn't know. She didn't know why, breathlessly, she said, *I don't want to go home.*

THE MEETING

SHE COULD LIVE ON MY street. I would pass her on my evening walk, or see her at the drugstore, or at the grocery store that smells of the tropics, in the interminable lineup at the cash. I would break the ice, *What a glorious, sunny day!* She would turn her head towards me, look at me, finally look at me. I would take on a form in the abyss of her eyes, a physical form, and she would answer without the hint of a smile, *Yes, it's a beautiful day*. She would become a woman with a voice, carrying in its wake the traces of a dormant sorrow. Dormant? Is that really so? Perhaps, in the middle of a sentence, soldiers appear to her, the odour of blood and shit clinging to their boots, and the cries of her father whose throat is being cut.

But I am dramatizing, still making things up, as I wait for the metro, leaning against a graffiti-covered column. This young woman must have been born here, with a cab driver for a father, and a mother who is ruining her eyes by the light of an inferior sewing machine. She doesn't have time to notice that the little girl is lonely, so lonely, locked inside her body as in one of those shelters rich people had built for themselves in the days of the Cold War. She is waiting for the metro, too, pacing up and down, every day at the same time, with the same scarf, the same large, dirty raincoat, even though it's June, the same inarticulate mumblings between her teeth. I think of going up to her, slowly, so as not to frighten her. I get closer. I speak to her, softly, and the miracle happens. She answers me.

But I have never dared, and she remains a fictional character. I can keep wondering where she is going, every day, in the early afternoon. Perhaps to a drop-in centre for people like her, a kind of refuge run by a church whose name I don't know, some sect that mixes Christian rites with pagan ones. There are so many sects that comfort immigrants. One of these days I might shadow her — I dreamt of becoming a private eye when I was a teenager. I would follow her out of the metro, tail her to the far end of the city if necessary. But I needn't worry, we both get off at the same downtown station. Is she enrolled at the university, perhaps? I think that's impossible, but my companion says she is. She is quite a sight as she paces up and down in her dirty coat, which completely covers up her body. She is getting enough to eat, though. Big shoulders, round cheeks. In fact, she has put on weight lately.

The train. We both hurry inside, and I drop into the orange seat, right in front of the one she takes, while I try to catch her eye. She won't look at me. She sees no one. She is alone, as in her childhood. As alone as one can be when one remembers too much. Remembers what? I barely have time to ask myself the question, distracted by an elderly couple getting up. The train enters a station, slows down. The doors open, discharging the old people onto the platform. Arm in arm, they inch their way towards the exit. They are holding their own against their fate. So will I, at their age. I smile — now that my daughter is expecting a child, I am forever picturing myself as a little old lady. Is that ridiculous? Well, anyway, I no longer feel that I have my whole life ahead of me. Actually, a woman my age is entering the car with a beautiful, young, dark-haired woman who looks so much like her she must be her daughter. They take turns keeping a baby in a stroller amused with a rattle. It's a quiet, friendly little boy, a cherished child.

Around us, all eyes are riveted on little Raphaël. The grandmother just mentioned his name. He bursts out laughing while his mother wipes the dribble off his chin. Magical, the laughter of a child. Some people would find this scene kitschy. Too bad for them. I need small joys. I am becoming vulnerable as I get older. I feel more and more powerless when I skim through the newspapers in the morning.

With squeals of glee, Raphaël looks at the rattle he has thrown on the floor. I bend down to pick it up. My gaze meets the wild eyes of the woman in the raincoat. Then she turns her head towards the child as if she is puzzled by so much delight, love, and attention for such an insignificant creature. Yes, she was left completely on her own as a child. I am sure of it now. A wave of anxiety comes over me. How can I describe the feeling? It washes over me at every turn, as though the slightest joy awakened all the sorrows of the world. But it's a feeling of injustice, rather. Something more disturbing than compassion. A needle slowly piercing the skin, being thrust between the ribs, lodging itself in the heart.

I hold out the rattle to the grandmother. She takes it, thanking me. The baby gives me an irresistible smile. I feel happy again. My grandson, too, will love to babble, and laugh, and play. I can't do anything about the woes that plague the world, but I can do something to help my grandson. What's the use of giving in to despair? We must get moving, do something, think of the future. The young mother now puts the bonnet back on the baby's head, and he gets angry. The women push the stroller towards the doors. The train slows down. I look for the name that will soon appear. I have totally lost track of the time. Only two more stations — I won't be late for the meeting. I am eager to leave behind the young woman, who still has a vacant look in her eyes.

The conductor closes the doors, but reopens them at once. Who is the idiot who is having fun blocking them? The doors close once more, but only to open again. Disappointed frowns appear. *A technical problem*, the conductor announces over the loudspeaker. Fortunately, it isn't an incident, as attempted suicides are called. I had better make the best of it. I take an essay out of my bag. With a little bit of luck, I won't be delayed too much. I try to immerse myself in a colleague's reflections on the future of the novel. I almost succeed, drawn gradually into perceptive observations on fiction and reality.

I forget about the young woman, about little Raphaël, his grandmother, humanity's problems.

Then a slow snap. A passenger beside me heaves a sigh of relief. The doors are closing again. The chime sounds, and we are off. My gaze drifts towards the young woman in front of me. Still motionless, wild-eyed. She has removed her coat. She is wearing a maternity dress. I stare at her, transfixed. This is the one thing I never, ever imagined. I wonder if I'll be able to pull myself together over the next two stops, to take my eyes off that stomach, pick up my bag, leave the station, and go and talk at that meeting about our everyday affairs.

II

A CERTAIN LAUGH

In memory of Louise Lefaivre

IT'S A FEMALE. YOU ARE unable to take your eyes off the hardened teats that will never have suckled. The dog was too young, eight or nine months at the very most. Even lifeless, the body retains the gracefulness of childhood, just as with humans. You think so, but, unlike your great-grandmothers, you have never lost a child. The only dead child you have ever seen was a little girl in Palermo, in the catacombs of the Capuchins, who, embalmed according to forbidden processes, had been smiling in her white coffin for nearly a hundred years. The sight of her didn't make you sad. The little girl looked like a doll laid down in her cradle.

The bitch looks like death, though. The open mouth baring sparse teeth, the yellow fur stuck to the flanks, her body contorting as it lifts with each wave. The sea advances. The sea invades. The sea spits out its refuse on the beach — shells, mouldy seaweed, empty Coca-Cola bottles, dogs that have drowned or were beaten to death with pebbles perhaps. Impossible to know. You will never find out what happened to the little dog. What difference could it make in your life, really? But you would like to find a cause, a motive. Although you dream of the sea as it is pictured in cheery songs, the image of the stiffened body will not let go of you.

Before, you would never have such thoughts, or else they simply would have flitted across your mind, and you would have managed to dismiss them straight away. What you used to see, on the beach, was life, lazy and long, as you watched young people who don't yet protect themselves from the sun. Well hidden under your parasol, you already belong to another age. That's the way it is. Time flies. You are beginning to understand this trivial phrase. Yes, you have started uttering platitudes. All it took was a message on your computer screen one night, and time froze in the now bluish veins of your hands. You copied down the address of the funeral parlour. Then, dry-eyed, you turned off the machine.

You were expecting it. That is to say, you knew the time was near, as one does when a child is about to be born. Destiny would take its course. Every night, there was a new message on your screen. Every night, she had deteriorated a little more. A few days earlier, at the hospital, you had barely recognized her under her oxygen mask. Already her face looked like that of a drowned woman. Fortunately, there were her eyes, still bright, and there was her voice, detached from her sick body, talking calmly about the final arrangements. Unintentionally you found yourself agreeing. Yes, yes, that music and those speakers were suitable. Why hesitate? The need to hear the word *tomorrow* ring out, the need to imagine a future when one will be present even though absent, the hope of living on for others until they die, too — that is probably how it is, at the very end. Probably.

For the moment, you have not reached that point. This morning the sea rolls its foam across the sand and you watch it, motionless, in your beach chair, indulging in your friend's dream of immortality. You'd almost think she was still alive. You hear her laugh, as you did last summer. Had you sent her a postcard from Vienna or Prague on your holiday? You can't recall. These details were unimportant last year — you didn't know that all was lost. Or perhaps you chose not to read the signs of the inevitable in her face.

Afterwards, we ask ourselves what we would have done if we had known. Then, to avoid feeling remorseful, we say to ourselves that if we were condemned, we'd want others, those around us, to reflect back to us the image of a woman who is going to live. Yes, lack of concern is better than pity, no matter how benevolent. Besides, weren't you told that even while preparing her funeral she still had hope, like those miners trapped underground who had held out for seventeen days by drinking their own urine? You remember how that story disgusted you as a child. You would have chosen to die instead, you had said. And you still believe that, because it seems to you that life doesn't thrust its roots very deep into the fibres of your being. But how can you tell? Sometimes, indifferent or desperate people, when grappling with illness, suddenly show an intense desire to fight.

The light is magical this morning. Milky and heavy, a little opaque, as on the morning after a great storm. One feels like plunging into it, body and soul, and drifting, believing that death doesn't carry everything away, but leaves us something of those we lose. A thought, love, protection. Or just the memory of a laugh, a joyful, resounding laugh, like that of your friend.

You remember her last smile. She was happy to see you, at the hospital, because she wanted to say her farewells. And although you aren't good at talking, you tried hard, for once. It was now or never. You chose your words carefully. You weighed them before offering them, like the plain, solemn flowers women bring to seamen's chapels on Sundays. Discreet, yet deeply felt words. She knew. Didn't she reply that she was sorry you hadn't met sooner? You merely nodded. What was the use of adding regrets to regrets?

As if the same thought had crossed her mind, she turned her eyes towards the window and fastened her gaze on the dazzling Sunday sun. The day before, she had asked to go outside. They had pushed the bed along the corridor and into the tiny hospital garden, where she wanted to admire the blooming shrubs one more time. She was slipping away, but left you this image of herself: a woman, already tied to the bed where she would lose her life, who removes her mask for an instant to inhale the fragrance of the roses. And you said to yourself that in the final moments everything should blend together: sadness, happy memories, the scent of flowers, and shadows from the light on one's skin.

You look out at the sea while thinking of those in your circle who no longer do so. You think of the obituary columns in the newspaper, which your aunts pore over every morning. One day, you will reach that stage, too. But you have many years left. In your family, people die of old age. *Good genes*, your doctor told you. Your friend will not have been so fortunate, though. You would almost feel guilty, but what can you do about it?

You try to absolve yourself while you walk towards the body of the little dog, after hesitating for a long time. Strangely enough, you have to see her again. You need to face that tiny body so you can truly begin the new day. You couldn't stop thinking about her yesterday. The stiffened teats, the yellow hair washed by the brine: perhaps the body has begun to decay. Or the sea may have taken it back, swallowed it, offered it as a sacrifice to some nameless monster. You push the legends of the ancient world to the back of your mind, however. You are on an island that has many tourist attractions, developed for people like you, who want to forget their worries.

And yet your memory will not give you any respite. It follows you, quietly, and you don't run away from it. You take the time to stop. Here, there is only the sea. The sea that eases pain, that allows the living and the dead to meet. The sea is so beautiful — I wish you could see it! This is what occurs to you. This is what you would write to your friend if she could read your words. A trite sentence, yet the only sentence vast enough to embrace all of one's visions of the sea.

You are close to the village now. You walked all that distance without noticing, and you didn't see your little dog. You are almost relieved. In your memory, she will be intact, spared. But suddenly four young, yellow dogs, identical to the little bitch, appear. They surround you, yapping joyfully, and then — you don't know why — they take off and start running, running like mad towards an invisible point on the horizon. If they had a good memory, they wouldn't care about competitions. It's no use racing when the fifth one of the litter has already taken first place. But they have forgotten. Or perhaps they pretend they don't know.

SLEEPLESS NIGHT

PAIN. NOT A PAIN THAT shatters your skull. Uneasiness, rather. Subtle, nagging, like a soft light, which doesn't blind you but prevents you from dozing off. I didn't sleep a wink all night. Exhausted from tossing and turning in my sheets, I went and planted myself at the window to wait. Wait for what? An angel, a ghost, a miracle, a vision, a sign from heaven allowing me to understand ... yes, *understand*, that is all. One doesn't vanish one fine day without a trace. Even the vilest murderers leave clues behind. But not she. Nothing unusual in the house, no sign of a struggle. No article of clothing abandoned on the riverbank, no letter either.

A week already. Lethargy. And insomnia. I fall into a heavy sleep, and then always the same nightmare. She is there, beside me, sitting on the edge of my bed, in a white nightgown, her hair dishevelled, her breath on my neck, and her hands around my throat. I can't breathe. I wake up screaming. I get up. I stumble down the long wooden staircase and go and stand at the window. The reassuring sound of the waves lulls me. Only the waves can calm me down.

I refused to return to Québec with Paul yesterday, though he begged me to come with him. My heart is here, and my guts, and my life. For the moment. This madness won't last forever. I will recover my wits. We are bound to find out something. One of these mornings, the river will wash the body ashore, a hiker will find it in the forest, or Madeleine will materialize just as suddenly as she disappeared, all smiles, *It's me. How are you?* Perhaps she has simply gone away, on an impulse, as an angry gesture against me or Paul. It wouldn't be the first time. She vanishes like a genie in a story, but a few days later there is a phone call, a postcard. Paul and I finally got used to it.

I am lying. We haven't got used to it. I haven't, not this time anyway. How can you leave an isolated house in the forest if you have neither a car nor a motorbike? *She has more than one trick up her sleeve*, Paul says. I agree, I do, but there are limits to what is plausible. I shouldn't have got worked up, shouldn't have shouted. Paul withdrew into himself. He went to sit down on the riverbank. Once again I had talked too much. When would I learn to keep my feelings to myself? Paul no longer expects anything from Madeleine. He has been saying so for ages. In other words, he expects everything from her, even the irreparable. But is that really so? He is her father, after all. He has seen this woman being born, suck at her mother's breast, soil her diapers. He has seen her cry, laugh, say her first words, sleep through the night, teethe, do her homework, make her first mischief.

I am cold. A thin mist on the window. Soon, the first rays of the sun. The night will be swept up into the effervescence of the day. The telephone will ring. Paul. He will ask me if I slept. I will lie to him. What's the use of waving my fears like flags? Life must slowly settle back into place: work, desire. I will get out my canvases and brushes today. I will try to start a new painting, an abstract showing my distress, my anger, my immeasurable anger, aroused by Madeleine's immeasurable cruelty. She knows very well what she is inflicting on us: worry, fear, terror, dizzy spells, feeling the ground give way under our feet. There is nothing worse than not knowing, than telling ourselves the most dreadful things all day long, than the shadow of madness approaching, growing, threatening to swallow us up.

But she won't have our hide. That's what Paul and I vowed to each other yesterday, after making love. For the first time. We had to start doing it again, the body existing once more, outside the anguish. A patiently drawn horizon. A small joy. We mustn't go under. We mustn't. Madeleine won't have our hide. This is what we keep telling ourselves whenever Madeleine disappears. Especially Paul. How can he accept that he is powerless to help his daughter? I am too, for that matter. Although I haven't carried her in my womb, I have been Paul's wife for so many years now, I no longer count them. I have helped Madeleine study for her school exams, helped her prepare documents for job applications. I have known all her teenage loves. I have taken her in, comforted her, listened to her when she was sad. I am the stepmother, am I not? What a terrible word! What an ungrateful role! For Madeleine, there is only Paul, Paul, Paul, Paul. Everything is decided before the age of six, books tell us. At that time, I was stuck in one of my previous lives.

A few sunbeams now. They warm the river, caress the lawn, reach me through the window, bathe me. After the pitch-black night, here is the reign of the day. I will carry out the tasks of millions of women today: I will tidy up, go to the village to do some shopping, prepare a nice meal for myself tonight, have a glass of red wine, weed the rockery, pick herbs from the garden, listen to music, paint. Perhaps Madeleine will decide to reappear today. I don't know if I'll collapse or slap her so hard it will break her jaw. Will I be able to control myself? I can't say. I have replayed the scene a dozen times in my head, but I still don't know. I will not open my arms to her. Not this time. I am worn out, like an old dress. I don't have the inexhaustible reserve of love that Paul has. I am not the mother. I say *love*, I mean *guilt*. Is it Paul's fault that his wife took off one day, leaving her daughter behind the way one abandons a cat? No matter how often I tell him, I always have to start over again.

Paul has given his daughter everything: time, attention, ballet lessons, tennis lessons, swimming lessons, Spanish lessons, a private school, trips — everything. But a mother's abandonment leaves a hole in the heart, which gets bigger as the years go by. Nothing can fill it. I ought to know. I tried, at first. Madeleine soon put me in my place. I would remain her father's wife, a stranger, a rival she had to put up with.

Things have changed over time. I don't know what I mean to her today, but she knows how to find me when she needs me, and Paul, too, come to that. Madeleine is totally consumed by her torment. We cannot do anything for her. We are powerless spectators of her suffering as we watch her staring into space for long periods of time. Every so often she yells the worst insults at Paul. He doesn't reply, though. *But you can see she's not well*, he says. Of course she's not well, but we should do something, it seems to me, set limits, make it clear to her that we exist, too. We cannot let her rule the roost.

Always the same scenario: I try to stay calm but end up losing my temper, I blame myself, Paul feels alone with his sorrow, he suffers, I suffer seeing him suffer. It spreads like a microbe, a virus that invades the cells, causes physical pain, yes, pain. *She will make us ill in the end*, I say to Paul, sobbing. It isn't just a figure of speech. Sometimes, Paul cries too, and I promise I won't flare up again, I will be mindful of his feelings, we will be mindful of each other's feelings. Let's not make things more difficult, let's not allow ourselves to be destroyed by Madeleine. Be strong. Be brave. Help Paul. I promise, I promise.

It's incredible how Madeleine is wearing us out. Old soles that have trudged over stony roads. This image came to me in a dream. At the beginning of our love affair, Paul and I walked on and on, and the farther we walked, the deeper we plunged into a dense forest. Not a ray of light. Darkness. Fear. I cried for help, but no one could hear me. I woke up in a sweat that morning. And, for the first time, I asked myself how many couples in our predicament have broken up. Perhaps that is what Madeleine wanted: to get her father back, have him all to herself, but that wouldn't suit her really. It would be of no use to anyone. I would know how to employ cunning, to resist. I would hold out. I would know how to protect us, but I couldn't do it alone.

Paul and I are still together. We have asked for help. That's no disgrace. Other parents have too. There is so much suffering one doesn't see. People hide it. They try to take their minds off it. Can one blame them? This is something I will have learned, through Madeleine. To live with pain, as if it were a second skin. Or an incurable disease. But does one ever learn? I am more and more like Madeleine. I tell myself stories. I make things up. I only need to look in the mirror. Whenever she disappears, I waste away. Even a stranger would notice. One day, perhaps, I will no longer worry. Madeleine will find out, and won't enjoy vanishing into the countryside anymore. She will finally admit that she is ill. She will seek help. That's what Paul and I keep telling ourselves, for hope's sake. We don't live in the nineteenth century. There are so many possibilities nowadays. Madeleine will co-operate. She will.

But nothing is less certain, people say. She may always refuse. She may flaunt her pain until she dies. Or she may put an end to it herself at some point. In her own time. That's what I think. Would we recover? I have been trying to dismiss the thought all week, but each day it implants itself more firmly in my head. In Paul's too, I'm sure. We haven't spoken about it. We have learned not to express all our fears to each other. We would end up living in terror, fragile, ready to crumble. We must try to keep our spirits up, we mustn't cultivate a vision of gloom and doom.

We mustn't. We must. Always that verb on our lips, supplanting all others. My vocabulary is diminishing, like me. Shrinking away, like the wild ass's skin in that novel by Balzac. A little ass. I am a little ass. I haven't even unpacked my canvases. To think we rented this house so I could paint! But nothing presents itself to my view. The river is impossible. It only conjures up blackness, the blackness of sails announcing a death in ancient legends. And I say no. Not death. A white sail, rather, which would slowly detach itself from the foam of the river. Send us a sign, Madeleine, a tiny sign, and my anger will drop, I promise. It has already dropped, don't you see? You can come back. I'm waiting for you, I'm waiting for you. We can't bear to wait for you any longer. Even the dog. Rolled up into a ball, she now only goes out to do her business.

Day has broken, but the light is impenetrable. A fog thick enough to cut with a knife presses up against the screen. The landscape has disappeared. The garden, too. Only the house remains. Its straight, well-designed walls, the door frames, the windows hidden by foliage, and I, standing straight and still, my eyes fixed on a blurred point, from where a miracle might yet emerge. *It's miraculous to have to go back to work*, Paul said yesterday before he left. He must be up now. Was he able to get any sleep last night? He will arrive at the office looking gloomy, but he'll have to put on a cheerful face, and he will. Soon, he'll be caught up again in day-to-day problems — impatient customers, delivery dates, the employees, orders that aren't coming in. What he found intolerable in June will seem like a blessing. Anything to erase the image of Madeleine. Anything to forget. As for me, I won't start teaching again until September. For a month I will be plagued by memories, living memories of Madeleine, her auburn hair, the golden freckles on her bare arms, and her voice.

It is nearly eight o'clock. Paul is going to call. He'll tell me that he had a good trip in spite of the rain, that he found the house just as we had left it. As soon as the weather clears up, he will mow the lawn. *Everything's fine, everything's fine*, he'll keep saying to buck himself up. *With me too, me too*, I'll answer.

I will be telling the truth. I'll start a painting today. A black one because everything looks black to me. But never mind, I am going to paint. It will be my black period. Until once again I penetrate the secret of light.

SOMEWHERE ELSE, NEW YORK

IT IS HIS GAZE THAT draws her — a dense, foreign, Jewish gaze, she thinks while he approaches to congratulate her. A fine speech, really. How long has she been interested in the Middle East? She is about to reply that she has ended up here by a curious combination of circumstances. A guest cancelled at the last moment. The organizer was looking for a specialist in international law and persuaded her to take part in this forum. But he already turns his head away in the direction of a journalist who asks him for an interview.

She wanders off, offended. She takes a glass from a tray held out to her and walks towards a group of which she has met a few members. She will stay briefly and slip away. No one will notice her absence in any case. This reception bores her. The little incident has upset her, yet there was nothing unusual about it, as she keeps telling herself while giving clichéd answers to the people she talks to. She could have waited until the journalist had finished his interview. Why behave like a teenager? But he asked her a question out of pure politeness, and she would have liked him to pay attention to her, just for a moment or two, to feel that he didn't think of her simply as one more human form in this anonymous room.

She is heading towards the cloakroom when he catches up with her. Can't she wait a few minutes while he finishes the interview? They could have dinner together in a quiet restaurant, have a chat. He found her perspective fascinating. He wants to tell her again. She shakes her head. It is too late to redeem what has been ruined. She says she has an appointment, holds out her hand — they'll meet again at some other forum, there are sure to be opportunities to see each other in the future. She decides to walk home. That will help her regain her calm. She will make herself a ham sandwich, which she'll bolt while taking a hot bath, then nestle in her bed to finish the essay she started the previous night. And switch off the light early.

She does in fact switch it off early, after swallowing a sleeping tablet, and sinks into a dreamless sleep. The next morning, the telephone wakes her. She reads eight-thirty on her watch and picks up the phone, her mind still in a daze. It takes her a few seconds to recognize his voice. It's him. He has managed to get her number through the organizer. He absolutely wants to see her before returning to his country. He stresses *absolutely*. Would she give him the pleasure of her company this evening? She accepts without taking the time to think it over. What has she got to lose, after all? At worst, she will be bored to death. She wonders what to wear, though. Her black outfit would probably be too dressy. The beige dress is better — she won't look as if she is trying to be alluring.

He arrives at seven, as planned. She suggests they have an aperitif while deciding on a restaurant. He sits down in the leather armchair, asks for a whisky. She is stunned. How dreadful! Wouldn't he rather have a martini, a beer, or a glass of red wine? He bursts out laughing. *Aren't there any Québécois who drink whisky? Why is that?* She doesn't know. She ventures a reply: perhaps because the word sounds English. But he reminds her that gin is very popular here, and she admits defeat, she really doesn't know. Now they are talking as if they have known each other for ages. He is so glad that she agreed to see him again, he remarks while holding her gaze. Again, she notices his eyes — limpid, striking. Isn't it surprising, such pale eyes? *My father's eyes. I inherited them*, he explains, looking moved all of a sudden.

They have finished the aperitif, and not picked a restaurant yet. She mentions it, but he suggests they have another drink. Why leave straight away when they have only just broken the ice? Yes, why? *Why not eat here?* she says, a meal they'll throw together, a pasta dish with a salad? They'll open a bottle of wine and continue their quiet chat. The idea delights him — he has been staying at a hotel for a week. They head towards the kitchen. She gets out the saucepans. What a peculiar evening! Suddenly, she is bustling about with a stranger who offers to cut the vegetables as if he lived there. She watches him roll up his shirt sleeves and tie on an apron. She is amazed, really — thrilled, yet also fighting back her giggles. To think that yesterday he was only a name on a program to her.

Why is she smiling? he asks. She tells him straight out, and he starts laughing too. *We look like a couple that has just come home from work.* The word *couple* gives her a start. An innocent metaphor? Or does the word carry its full meaning? What desire do those liquid eyes conceal? And how should she react if the question came up? She just doesn't know. She furtively watches the man's bare forearms. She would like to be held in those arms. At least, she thinks so, but she has no way of knowing. Can a woman ever be sure of the effect of hands sliding over her shoulders, of palms moulding themselves for the first time around the curves of her hips, the very first moment, when she doesn't know yet if her body will acquiesce?

He puts the knife down on the table and asks if he can be of any more help. Everything is ready. There is nothing left for him to do but to pour himself a glass of wine and wait for the pasta. He remains standing, leans against the counter. He looks at her while she watches the burner, the fork in her hand. She feels he is studying her and, flustered, she pretends to be engrossed in what she is doing. There is silence. They should try to go back to laughing, but she can't think of a phrase that would dispel the uneasiness in the room. It's as if they had entered a corridor without an exit. He makes the decision to break the silence. *You know that you seem unreachable.* He has not missed his mark. She turns around abruptly. He is reminding her of the qualifiers people often apply to her: distant, enigmatic, mysterious. Should one surrender, bound hand and foot, at the first meeting, then? In a tense voice, she says, *Unreachable? No. Reserved, at the most*. He screws up his eyes and utters slowly, as if to himself, *Reserved? Perhaps. Perhaps so, after all*.

Here we are, the spaghetti is al dente. She is only too happy to deflect the conversation. She can serve now. Would he mind bringing the plates into the dining room? They sit down and eat. They are starved. The mood lightens. She questions him about his childhood. He opens up. He gets carried away. She listens. She realizes she has never imagined the life of a Jewish child. The evening is taking shape. They sit there, face to face, and, in that togetherness, their familiar selves emerge.

He falls silent. Perhaps the conversation no longer matters to him. He lifts the glass to his lips and looks at her as if he hadn't seen her yet. She can't explain why she moves her hand towards his, strokes it with her fingernail without saying a word. A distance between them is being bridged. They stay like that, touching each other lightly, until he pushes his chair back and goes up to her. They'll have only a few hours, he says. She doesn't dare tell him she had been sorry all day that she'd agreed to see him. Suddenly, the world is turned upside down. She rests her head on the shoulder that is offered. Reeling, she seeks his lips and leads him to the bedroom.

He talks on and on as he undresses her, and her body recognizes him. From where, she doesn't know. He knows the words that draw her out of herself. She responds to his voice, she sways in his arms, lets herself go.

He is quiet now, while she strokes his hair. Everything has been said. Through the half-open window, the sound of a Boeing reaches them, to bring them back to reality more quickly, perhaps. Will she see him again? She doesn't ask herself the question. They go to get some fruit and wine. They talk again, the way one talks after lovemaking, when the boundaries between bodies have become a little blurred. They enter into each other's world, they want to find out everything. He has begun to caress her again while she sums up the situation of Québec. He smiles as he feels her quiver under his touch. Her hips arch, and she slides against him, presses her lips against his. He takes her more violently this time. He takes control, and she becomes a woman who allows a man to take control.

The evening gives them a sense of weightlessness. The time flies. At this hour tomorrow, they will be at a great distance from one another. He is the one who brings it up: may he spend this last night with her? She shakes her head. She feels unable to make coffee in the morning for a man who is getting ready to disappear from her life. It's better to part in a lighthearted way than a woeful one. Doesn't he think so? He disagrees, completely, but complies. He has no choice. She watches him going down the steps, slipping into a taxi, melting into the darkness.

Then she wanders back into the dining room. She smiles when she notices the salad — they forgot about it. She puts everything away, anxious to have the room look as it did before, to store the evening in a fictitious memory, to remember it only when she wants to indulge in outlandish imaginings. She falls asleep in fresh sheets that smell of lavender. The world is in order once again.

She gets up early in the morning. She'll go and work at the office today. No one is there on Saturdays, so she'll be able to make up for lost time. She isn't keen on staying in the empty apartment anyway. The day passes as days do when one tries not to think. She barely feels a dim pang of nostalgia now and then — his gestures when they made love, and his voice, his voice. Then she turns towards the window and glances at the high-rises. Cars are moving, passersby cross the streets, the city stretches away into the distance, as always. Daylight is fading. She will soon have to go home.

When she gets back, she takes a steaming-hot bath and changes her clothes. She is especially glad to have agreed to that dinner at the restaurant with an old friend. She is trying to remember the menu. She'll choose quail *à l'orange*. She is about to leave when the phone rings. She is tempted to let it ring, but changes her mind — an emergency, perhaps. As soon as he starts speaking, she recognizes him. He will be boarding in a few minutes, he misses her. She listens, taken aback. He will call her. He promises. He will write to her. They'll meet again before the end of the year, here or over there. Or somewhere else, New York perhaps. Around her, things take on substance. Every single thing. She wants to believe in lucky chance encounters.

They have to hang up. She picks up her bag and goes out. Night has fallen. The air is turning mild. She feels enveloped. She'll walk. As she passes a shop window, she notices her silhouette in a mirror. She stops, pulls a long face at herself.

No, she hasn't begun to die.

DREAM WORLDS

YOU DIDN'T SAY GOODBYE TO the bookseller. You slipped out, embarrassed, looking down. Spending all that time in front of the displays and then leaving empty-handed ...

Yet you knew what you wanted. One of those big books people read at bedtime, to help them fall asleep. But you stopped, you don't know why, under the sign Travel Guides and stood rooted to the spot. Then you lifted the cover of a hardback book, fastened your eyes on the colour illustrations, and entered the greatness of Rome. You needed to be sensible, though. You put Rome back on the shelf — your mother had never travelled. But straight away your hands reached for Athens, and Casablanca, and Tunis. You were off in a dream again.

You let the bus drive by without getting on. You are going to walk, slowly. Already the air is fragrant with the scent of lilies of the valley. People are beginning to stroll along the shops. You even notice a few customers at a sidewalk café. It's the kind of day when you feel like indulging yourself a bit. Why not take it easy for a little while? Perhaps an idea will come to you. How about giving your mother a piece of jewellery or a silk scarf? You always give her books. But no matter how thoroughly you search the shop windows, there isn't a single thing, a single little treat, that seems right. Your head is as empty as your hands.

What she wants is a book — you know her. You have bought her all of *Remembrance of Things Past*, volume after volume, then *Don Quixote*, right after *Kamouraska*. She stayed up very late to finish the biography of Gabrielle Roy, and even later to devour that of Marguerite Duras. She has imagined Babette's feast and, in English, lived the passionate love affair of the badly burned man. She has asked herself if she would have left Sartre for Nelson Algren. Then, after *The Words*, she made up her mind that Simone de Beauvoir had made the right decision.

Yes, you know what she likes, but unfortunately you were pulled in by that photograph of the coliseum in Rome, and suddenly everything changed. You thought of the coliseum at El Djem, of your trek across the desert, of Djerba, where Ulysses halted, and, deep inside, you felt the touch of the man you love. History blended with legend, real love with tales of bewitchment, but never mind, it all became real because you could look at the pictures with eyes that had seen those fabled places.

Your mother is happy in her house, as she tells you with a smile at each of your visits, and you have come to believe her. She isn't bitter like many people her age. You think she is still beautiful, and chic, and gracious. You will just have to believe her. Isn't that what you want, anyway? But every now and then you get an odd, sinking feeling in the pit of your stomach, and you say to yourself that she hasn't had the life that you have. A comment may slip out as she muses on the past, opening a gap in the flow of words. Then your childhood comes back to you. You see images that have never been photographed: your father's poor health, the money problems, and other ones, a pain barely hinted at. Then she returns to the present. But you remain trapped in the tangle of old worries that you gave up trying to unravel a long time ago.

Other women her age have led different lives. Not in the world of the dark-haired little girl you once were, a world where mothers were tightly laced into their motherly corsets. But you read too, after all. Love affairs, travelling, writing, dancing — it's all there, in black and white, in biographies. These are the women she likes to talk about, late at night, when dreams and reality begin to overlap. You asked her one day if she would have wanted to live the life of Gabrielle Roy, or that of Duras, or de Beauvoir, but almost instantly she had shaken her head, no, not those lives, they were too painful, too complicated. Reading about them was enough for her. And how about you? She hadn't asked you that. Yet you would have known what to answer. True, these women left great works behind, but you would have admitted that you wouldn't have wanted to find yourself in one of those lives either.

It isn't your fault that you lead the life of a modern woman — not always an easy one, with time broken up, time shaved off so as to gain a few hours, but your books do get written in the end, you manage to reflect on things, to laugh, to raise your glass high on festive occasions. You love someone, you are loved in return. You like to think that a wider path has opened for you now, a way of seeing the world, of coming to terms with the anguish that sometimes torments you, when the night turns shadows into ghosts. You like to think so, but, deep inside your fragile self, you sense that you may be wrong. Perhaps there isn't as much distance between you and your mother as you thought.

Tomorrow you will cross the river, and then the plain, which, after all these years, still looks foreign to you. Next, the road will plunge into mountainous rock, and you will find that dark-haired little girl again who will always be a part of you. Your mother will have come to meet you. You will have brought her a present as usual. You'll hold out a book to her. Yes, a book. Already you retrace your steps. You are returning to your bookstore.

You go in. You call out a ringing hello in spite of the blush on your cheeks. You tell the owner you forgot to get a text for your courses. She knows you well — she pretends to believe you. You will be able to browse as long as you need to. You steer clear of the shelf with the travel guides and head straight for the fiction section. You have made up your mind. This time you'll choose the life of a woman who has never existed. It may take a while, but you are sure you will find something.

OLD-FASHIONED WORDS

THAT SUMMER THE WORLD LIT up again. She didn't want to ask herself why. She would rather continue living in a kind of blindness, completely unaware. It was summer, the heart of summer, a time for the beach and birdsong. And she walked along, heading I don't know where, towards that tiny, buried kernel that keeps us rooted to the earth. She had only glanced at the letter he had sent her, just barely noticing the words, which seemed strange to her. She wasn't paying attention. She appeared detached from it all. I loved to see her like that. I loved her, I mean to say, and I simply wanted to see her happy, as though it were possible for a whole new life to emerge from her old one. I have always been immensely naive and don't hide that very well. Sometimes I feel a little ashamed of it at receptions, where one is supposed to put on a disillusioned expression. It's the side of me that has aged the least, my hidden face, in a way, which suddenly reveals itself in the middle of a sentence, when old-fashioned words, *love*, *hope*, *happiness*, are used — words that make ugly blots in the conversation.

All winter long she had been so withdrawn that I had felt extremely worried. What was happening between him and her? No one really knew, but I noticed there was trouble.

Oh, no clear signs, no obvious facts. Just vague hints, a certain doubt in their eyes when they watched one another, as if, after all those years of living together, they didn't recognize each other anymore. He no longer murmured the pet names one gives to a lover, and she didn't seem to realize it. She had become oblivious to others, as when she looked at me without seeing me if I asked her a question. She was slipping away from me, avoiding me, and yet I didn't feel I was losing her. We would manage to find each other again. She was my mother and always would be.

He showed up one fine Saturday in July, after the holidays. Mama had met him I don't know where, and now he came to spend a few days at our house, with that fake casual air of his. I think I understood straight away that he was in love with Mama and would do everything he could to snatch her from me. I felt hatred for him, pure hatred, the hatred of a child who knows she won't win. My mother behaved with him as I had never seen her behave before. She would languorously lay her hand on the nape of his neck when she talked to him, or smile at him in a particular way while she brought a dish to the table. It was hell at our house, a hell of love. He adored us both, he said as he kissed us, and he wanted to come and spend all his weekends with us.

It was only after I left home that I noticed he really was fond of me. During all those years that we lived under the same roof, I hadn't realized it, even though he helped me with my homework, even though he never missed a school play in which I had a part. In reply to girls who asked me, *Is that your father?* I would vigorously shake my head. The idea! With me so dark and him so fair! But I had got used to him being there, as one gets used to an incurable, but not fatal, disease. I hadn't lost my mother, after all. She was still there for me. Besides, I had grown up. In my pockets I carried photos of movie stars I dreamed about and one of a boy, a real one, whom I'd met during a school-exchange trip. Time was stealthily doing its work.

I last heard from him three years ago. He called me to tell me he had signed a contract with a development agency. He didn't know yet to what African country they would send him. He didn't really care, anyway — between him and my mother, things weren't going well at all. I didn't cry when I hung up. I had too many worries of my own. I had been unemployed for nearly three months and held out little hope of finding work. Besides, my mother had become a shadow of her former self. A decision had to be made.

Relieved is actually the word that might best describe my reaction. But not just relieved. My mother would belong to me again. I would have her all to myself, as in the past. I asked her to come and spend a few weeks with me. I would cook tasty dishes for her, take her to the movies. At first, she refused. I had to plead my case. Then she arrived one evening with enough clothes for two or three weeks. I had succeeded. I was as happy as when I got a medal after a figure-skating event at the local sports centre.

She stayed for two months. In the beginning, she kept a mournful silence. When she came back from work, she turned on the television and left it on all evening. Then, little by little, she started chatting with me. I tried to cheer her up, and once in a while she caught herself laughing, she would briefly forget her sorrow. But often she remembered, and tears rolled down her cheeks. Her image was cracked. She had nothing more to hide. And I needed her fragility in order to assert my own strength. Did she sense that? Perhaps, because she, who had always been so discreet, began to confide in me.

We never picture our mother in the role of a lover, even when we know she has been in love. We never picture our mother like other women, as if — thanks to a blackout of our knowledge — she were protected from the harrowing human condition. I discovered she was similar to me: fragile, hesitant, unable to deal with the blow she had suffered. Like me, the previous year, when Martin and I parted.

When she went home, summer had truly arrived and she had begun to eat again. I had stopped addressing her as Mama. I now called her by her first name, Monique. This is a difference between the generations: Grandmother never had a given name again after her marriage. Oddly enough, it took this spell of unhappiness for my mother to start acting younger. She had her hair cut, exchanged her house for an apartment with a skylight, began to talk about travelling. She still thought about him once in a while, she said, but only as a tranquil memory. I had grown peaceful, too. Martin was going to get married. My heart had almost given way when I heard the news, but I had survived. Three years ago, already.

This afternoon, the rounded forms of the trees are silhouetted against the light. I hold Jean-Philippe's hand as we stroll along, thrilled with the great news we are about to give Monique. I am pregnant. When we walked past my childhood school, I thought of him, I don't know why. I would have liked him to know, too, deep in the heart of his Africa.

FUNERAL

ONE DAY, YOUR FATHER IS no longer your father, but a lifeless body, a corpse, like your grandfather.

It all happened in an instant. The ringing of the telephone, your brother's voice, the voice of a man who isn't good at talking, and you answered, *I'll be there tonight*, your eyes on the alarm clock. Was it too early to let the college know?

Without a trace of emotion you heard yourself say to the dean, *My father has died*. He offered you his condolences. You automatically thanked him. Your mind was on the exam questions you needed to prepare for your students. And you had to find a supply teacher, check the railway timetables, have your suit cleaned, and buy a new outfit for your son. But first break the news to him. How does one break such news to a ten-year-old child? You didn't have time to think of your father. You didn't have time to wonder if you had been in his thoughts when he died.

It would take a few days, perhaps a month. One night, your father would smile at you in his sleep, and that man wouldn't be the one who left you without saying a final goodbye, it would be another father, the father who used to tell you preposterous stories when you were small. Already then, you didn't take him seriously. But you liked his booming voice, and his laughter when there were no heroes or villains left, and you laughed along with him, although you knew real stories didn't end that way. People got married, lived happily ever after. They basked in a reassuring kind of contentment, with rewards and punishments. That world was orderly. Princes appeared at the right time.

You never imagined your father as a prince — with his dirty shirt when he came home from work, his callused hands, and that thick stubble, which, in the summer, he shaved off morning and night. You didn't recognize him in the picture your mother had framed and would look at every so often as if she were seeing it for the first time. He was handsome and young, and he smiled, but his smile was dimmed by sadness, or grief rather, as if, long ago, his life got caught in the cogwheels of misfortune, and he had needed to extricate it patiently. No doubt because he was an orphan.

Orphan was a word you heard at home even before you found out what it signified. *Orphanage*, too, the large school-like building crammed with hundreds of children. You never understood what it meant to have neither a mother nor a father, except one day when you saw a movie on television in which a little boy wandered along the roads of France in search of his parents. You sobbed your little heart out and then promptly forgot about it. All you know about your father's mother is her name, her first name, the one you were given at birth. Nothing else. That was all your father ever told you. That was all he knew. He only had a vague memory of her, a blurred, shadowy vision. He is on a ferry, his blond hair hidden under a tiny red toque, while a faceless woman holds his hand.

Now his hands are folded forever, his fingernails neatly clipped, like the nails of men who wear smart shirts to work and can speak without making mistakes. That is the kind of father you dreamed up for yourself when you were eleven. At nighttime, in bed, you closed your eyes and became the daughter of a man you were proud of — an insurance agent, a doctor, a lawyer. A father who would sit down at the table on Monday after supper and correct your Latin translations. Your own father was at work when you did your homework. He was a night watchman in a garage, where the hours slowly ticked away until the break of dawn, and all those hours on watch put end to end were an interminable ribbon, unrolling night after night, year after year. What could he be thinking about? His life didn't belong to you. You were asleep at night.

You wasn't just you, but your little brothers and you — a solid, indivisible unit, an entity nothing could shatter, not even in the everlasting future. You hadn't learnt to see yourself yet with eyes that scour the crevices of the heart in search of still waters, wintry scents, rites of mourning. You liked to play hopscotch or cowboys and Indians in the garden. You walked straight ahead in your world, expecting to be followed. You were followed, you were listened to, you were the oldest.

Then, one Saturday in February, there was blood between your legs, and you were alone all of a sudden, faced with a mystery you needed to carefully hide under white cloths. You were no longer a child, but a girl, for good. Deep inside your body, you would know the body of a man, the kicks of a child, feelings one cannot share. You left your brothers to their guns and started reading love stories. You would practise saying *I love you*, smearing your mouth with gaudy red lipstick in front of the bathroom mirror.

You have said *I love you* to several men. The tall, redheaded one you loved passionately at sixteen, who was to become your first lover, followed by others, whom you weren't sure you really wanted. But you were trying to reassure yourself when you opened your blouse. You said *I love you* as a magic formula, so they would answer, *Me, too*. You were never convinced that a man would open his arms to you.

Now there is your son, and the man close to you, and the life patiently built within your old life. You focus on a tiny rectangle in your head and fill it with promises. You don't look towards the past quite as often anymore. Your silence, the way you stroke the cold, makeup covered cheek, which doesn't shrink from your touch: you seem to have drawn a borderline between remembering and forgetting. You think so, anyway, as you kneel on the prayer stool, stirred by the rich smells of Mass, the face of the merciful Christ, the calls to holiness. At this particular moment, it all moves you deeply. You are engaged in trying to love your father.

But an aunt comes to sit with you, and you are instantly back in the thick of your old memories — the Sunday visits, the clean Sunday dresses. It really is Sunday all of a sudden. You are four years old. Your father is at home. You would like him to take you on his knee. Hasn't he been away every night of the week? But he is having a leisurely smoke and doesn't see you. So you shout, jump about, make a dreadful racket. At last he gets up, walks towards you, and gives you that slap that you will never forget. Never again will you ask him for a little love.

In the smoking room, you now listen to your aunt telling you stories from her younger days. You listen with only half an ear while you struggle to silence the anger within you, the bottled-up anger that creeps up your spine, reaches the back of your neck, and will soon settle in your jaws — a steely anger, like a secret you wouldn't dare confide to anyone. It's not your fault if you are incapable of mourning your father. How can you mourn a man you have never really known?

But you are asked a question and need to break your silence. You answer. You remain polite, after all. You talk about the present, the passing seasons. No, the man they met at your wedding is no longer your husband, and your son is growing up, he will soon be eleven, he already looks like a teenager in the jacket you bought him. You become a mother again, with a mother's concerns, and you say the things mothers say at funerals.

They come to get you because the coffin is about to be closed. You will spend a few quiet moments saying your last, obligatory, farewell. Then you will slip your arm through your mother's. You'll head towards the car that is going to take you to the church. You'll take a seat in the front row, where you'll get up, sit down, and kneel along with the rest of the family, and pretend to be praying. Perhaps you really will be praying, in your own way. You will be trying to close your childhood, as you kneel before the flowers and wafting incense. But it will reopen. You know that. And you will have to start all over again.

THE CAT

SHE LEFT HIM ONE NIGHT without a word, the way a woman leaves a man she has passionately loved, when she cannot bear to speak words that could kill. She didn't take anything with her, except the cat, a present he had given her for her birthday the previous year — an ugly, grey-and-white cat with eyes of different colours. While she put the animal in its cage, she recalled the afternoon when they had gone to buy it. She had pointed at the dreadfully ugly grey-and-white kitten, and he had hugged her, wanting to know why. Why that one? With a peal of laughter, she had defended herself. That one, because nobody would adopt it, it would end its days in a laboratory. He had kissed her temple — she remembered it perfectly — and she had kissed him back.

She closed the door behind her, incapable of uttering soothing phrases, *Take good care of yourself*, or, by way of explanation, *There is no other solution*. Her anger had subsided. She found herself in the darkness, a dreary darkness, without knowing where to go. It didn't matter, though, since she knew with absolute certainty that she would never see him again. How could she possibly see a man again whom she had loved so much? How could she make banal small talk after living through such a passionate love affair? She knew she wouldn't see him again and she didn't. She asked her friends never to mention him in her presence. She changed her cat's name. She lived the life of a woman who was trying to forget.

Then she decided the time had come for her to have a child. She had a child, a fair and rosy little boy, who didn't look like anyone she knew. She loved him for that reason — he didn't remind her of anything, he represented amnesia. She moulded her life around that child. It was a routine existence: games, meals, small sorrows, a closed, restricted world without emptiness. Sometimes her thoughts drifted back to him — the man she had loved so fiercely. Yet she couldn't visualize him, neither his face nor his hands. He had become a pure abstraction, although she did imagine certain scenes. What had become of him? Was he in love again — he who had told her one night that he would never be able to live without her? She tried to picture another woman in the bed where she had slept, the unchanged bedroom while the lovers kissed, the rustling of the poplar outside the window, the nasturtiums in the flower bed in the garden. But she felt no pain.

The cat was getting old. It no longer hunted, wouldn't go outside during the long winter months. At night, it snuggled up to her and purred. She would stroke it, speaking to it tenderly. The following summer, her son refused to go to the seaside with her. He wanted to go to camp, with boys his own age. She looked away, promised to think it over. In the mirror, that evening, she noticed a deep wrinkle at the corner of her lips. She had to face the facts: the child would grow away from her. He already was. She would do nothing to hold him back.

She drove him there herself. That's where she met *him*, with his son, whom he had driven there himself, too. She hadn't forgotten. The way he smiled, tilting his head to the side. His slightly hoarse voice. When he arranged to meet her, she agreed. She would see him again. Now.

Sitting on the terrace of the restaurant, she watches him coming, with that nonchalant walk of his. She observes him, alarmed. What will the evening bring, serenity or sorrow? But it's too late to change her mind. He is heading towards her. He is really happy to see her again, he says. She doesn't respond. What response can a woman make who hasn't forgotten anything? All she can do is accept to utter platitudes, *It's been such a long time*, phrases that allow them to edge their way towards one another in the heat of July.

It's been such a long time. She remembers the July evening, much like this one, when he told her for the first time that he was in love with her. She remembers the emotion, the silence that had followed, when he put his hand on hers, yes, the same emotion she feels right now as he whispers, lightly stroking her palm, that he will never forget her. How long will it be before she tells him she still loves him? The time it will take them to finish the meal perhaps, or one last liqueur? She doesn't know. She keeps silent for now. She watches him. Even though he has aged, he hasn't changed.

There are nights when two people don't want to remember the final words that were spoken. They dream of being happy as they smoke their cigarettes. They tell themselves that the wrinkles in the other's face are there simply by happenstance. They may have been mistaken about their feelings. There are nights when they don't want to say goodbye. Almost automatically, he asks her to come and spend the night at his house. And, almost automatically, she invites him over to her place instead. For now, she couldn't bear to see the house again ... the bedroom, the poplar in front of the window, the flower bed with nasturtiums. She doesn't want any landmarks, any reminders of the past.

She gives him the address. She'll drive slowly. He'll follow. There they are — they've arrived. A new neighbourhood, where he has never been. Yes, this is the place. He wraps his arm around her shoulders as they go up the few steps of the staircase. But she quickly frees herself, stifling a cry. The old grey-and-white cat is stretched out in front of the door. Already stiff, already cold.

ROOM 28

HE IS ASLEEP. ASLEEP AND smiling, his hands open, relaxed. She shivers. Already a chill in the air. She should close the window. She pulls the blanket over his shoulders instead. He is asleep and she observes him. She would like to brush the auburn lock away from his eyelid but doesn't dare make the slightest move. Above all, she mustn't wake him. She turns her eyes towards the window. The curtain no longer sways. The wind has dropped. Dawn is near. She thinks about the life she will soon go back to. She scans the sky for a ray of light. Still too early.

He is smiling. She envies him for being asleep while she, feeling too unsettled, hasn't slept at all. Will he cry, she wonders, when he wakes up? She recalls his tears, the desperate way in which he fondled her breasts. He almost shouted that he wanted her terribly in spite of that sudden impotence. She wasn't sure she fully understood his despair. They were together in this windy night, weren't they? Why be so dramatic? She took him in her arms and he fell asleep, calmed down, convinced perhaps that the voice whispering tender words to him was sincere.

Now the light shows through the curtains. Time to get up. She slips on her dress, goes over to the window, manages to close it quietly, and heads back towards the bed. She kisses his temple and smiles.

Nothing, no one, in the corridor. A row of identical doors. She checks to make sure her key is in her pocket and starts walking, looking for her room number. A pang of nostalgia all of a sudden. She wants to believe there will be other nights.

ALL-INCLUSIVE

YOU HAVE SOUGHT THE SEA in all the countries you have travelled through. You have seen it bristling, angry, towering, but most often drowsy, almost dozing, and what came back to you then was the image of that jam-packed lake where an aunt who had a car used to take you and your sisters. You love the sea in all its moods and make your way towards it every summer. You couldn't possibly get through a year without that salty smell on your skin. You go there as on a pilgrimage. You ask for a room from which you can contemplate it, and you spend long hours making peace with your life.

This year, a remote island highly praised by a travel agent. A wildlife sanctuary, crabs, giant turtles that come and lay their eggs on the beach, a few scattered hotels for tourists who waited too long to rent their dream house. You paid for the package and left, your small bag under your arm. And here you are, in solitary ecstasy, pacing up and down the deserted beach. Yes, it's almost deserted, the travel agent spoke the truth. At this time of year, the hotel is half empty and the guests don't come down until late morning. For the space of a walk, you can fantasize that the island is yours. Why not? You know of people who own palaces, ocean liners, and towns — nouveaux riches you wouldn't keep company with, but why not pretend this morning to be above the fray? A few minutes from now, at the briefing for newcomers, it will be time to come back to reality anyway.

The men and women here are just like you, in fact. Working people who have come to stock up on sunshine for the winter. All the easy chairs in the hotel lobby are taken. You politely greet your airplane seatmates of row seventeen, a couple of restaurateurs in their late forties you don't wish to socialize with, and your eyes scan the room while you accept the inevitable welcome punch from the tour representative. True, it's only ten o'clock, but these drinks are so diluted they could be poured into the bottle of that gurgling baby over there, in the shade of the tropical plant. Where is her parents' room? Far from yours, you hope, with a stab of guilt for being one of those single people who prefer cats to children. But this is your holiday. You haven't flown thousands of kilometres to feel you have landed up in a daycare centre.

And now it's time for some information that is essential for your stay, explains the representative, who seems rather businesslike. You wonder who she is — who these women are who've come to work in the south for a ridiculously low salary, no doubt — while she describes the practical details of your life in this establishment. Mealtimes, the bars, excursions, towels, the rules to be followed on the beach. You prick up your ears: she requests that the nudists stay far away from the families, at the farthest point of the foreshore, and the guests around you discreetly study each other, wondering, perhaps, whom they may run into stark naked. You lower your eyes, amused by the thought. You have visited hotels, even in Muslim countries, where European women sunbathe topless, but this is the first time you hear nudism mentioned in an all-inclusive resort.

The very centre of the beach. Activity coordinators coming to ask you to join the volleyball game. Children with spades and pink buckets. A few pedal boats rocking gently with the waves of low tide, and a sailboat overturning every fifteen minutes, making you wonder what masochist is going to so much trouble on his holidays while one can read wonderful novels or go and get an ice-cold drink at the tiny bar near the swimming pool. But everyone is entitled to their tastes — that huge woman, for example, who takes off her bra before she sets out for a walk, while she could quietly sunbathe under her beach umbrella without showing off her sagging breasts.

You, too, would like to walk around topless on the beach, but you don't dare. You have always been too aware of your appearance — the effect of advertising, of course, and also a remnant of modesty, because one doesn't go to convent school for all those years without something of it staying with you. You love this hotel: the decoration, the quiet, the staff, and the distinguished, unassuming guests. You said so yesterday to a couple of Finns who invited you to join them for dinner. Normally, at this hour, they are already stretched out on the beach, but today you don't see them. They must have decided to go on the highly recommended fishing excursion.

You aren't going to stir from here these two weeks. As soon as you get back, you'll have to accompany your employer on a sales trip through Asia, so you intend to stock up on energy. You just want to read, sunbathe, and get up once in a while to go for a swim, or a walk. Yesterday, you headed towards the left, where the three hotels of the island are lined up like fortresses. You made the rounds of the souvenir shops and then ordered your usual margarita in a different bar for a change of scenery. Today, you plan to walk towards the right. You'll cross the nudist beach so you can go and photograph the wilderness, even though you are a little afraid. It's perfectly safe, you've been told, but one never knows who may suddenly appear. Yet you won't stay rooted to the spot just because you are a woman on her own.

It all becomes more and more bare: the beach, the sea, and the vacationers. In just a few seconds you will pass that pot-bellied man with the nonchalantly dangling penis. You hardly recognize your neighbour from this morning's breakfast table, and his partner, a woman with yellow hair who doesn't shrink from displaying herself. You wonder if you should greet them or pretend you don't know them, but they quickly solve your dilemma with a hearty *Guten Tag*. You didn't think it would be quite so easy. A young woman near you laughingly smears a whitish cream on her partner. In the distance, a mature man makes his way towards the sea as slowly as a monk. You feel you have journeyed into the heart of tranquillity and ended up on a desert island.

You notice more and more people you say hello to at the bar, at the pool, or in the dining room. People of all ages. There are the Finns whose table you shared yesterday. They didn't go on the excursion. They are reading under a beach umbrella, a bit off to the side. From their discreetness, you gather this is their first visit to the nudist clan. They have been able to defy their taboos. You admire them. If you weren't so shy, you would slip off your bathing suit, too, and stretch out on the sand. You imagine the salt, the smell of the sea, the breeze, the caress of the breeze on your skin.

You don't feel like going to the dunes to photograph birds anymore. You must take the plunge right now because this afternoon you won't have the courage. You stroll back towards the nudists while trying to spot an empty chair in the third umbrella row. From there, you'll be able to observe the local customs. You won't make a blunder. You notice that not everyone is naked. In front of you, a beautiful Italian woman tries to persuade her companion to take off his bathing trunks, but he gleefully resists. A young woman plunges into the waves, with only her bikini bottom. Feeling more comfortable suddenly, you decide to copy her. One can proceed by stages, then. You unhook your bra and pick up a magazine so you will look at ease.

You would never have believed you were such a voyeur, but perhaps it's just the novelty. Most people come and go as in a cafeteria, while others, neophytes obviously, scurry about like frightened birds. There are exhibitionists, too. A stallion dozes with his legs spread apart so passersby can get a good view of his equipment, which is worthy of a porno film. Another man, farther away, paces back and forth in front of a group of women bathers. A voyeur you may well be, but you are ideally positioned to indulge your little perversions. You feel relaxed now. You even grow absorbed in an interesting article about the dangers of suntans.

The woman beside you starts rummaging in her bag. Getting more and more annoyed, she jumbles everything up, and then breathes a sigh of relief. She shows her partner a pair of tweezers and begins to pull out, one by one, the hair that's growing back on her vulva. How crude! Then you notice that all the women have white sexes, like infants. You will never get used to it. Actually, you have to fight with your aesthetician at each of your visits because she wants to wax your bikini line. And each time you repeat the same arguments. Why should you follow fashions that are dictated by men who are afraid of women? You like a thick fleece. You will never touch a hair of your auburn bush.

Oh well, this isn't the place to be militant. You fix your gaze on the horizon and try to forget about your neighbour, who is totally obsessed by her task. Besides, it's almost lunch hour, and time for the aperitif. You consider putting your bra back on and strolling over to the little bar near the swimming pool, when you recognize from behind your table companions who, their buttocks as white as the driven snow, are heading towards the sea. You could just slip off your bikini bottom and edge, like them, across the hot sand …

You don't cause a commotion. You take a big breath to the bottom of your lungs. You get up and start walking, holding your head high, trying not to blush. You walk on fearlessly. No one is watching you, except two or three voyeurs. But suddenly a shout. Then a woman's voice, *Did you see her? Couldn't she have shaved, at least?* And the entire beach turns towards your auburn fleece. People point at you. You are causing a real scandal. You walk faster and faster. You almost break into a run as you cover the ten metres between you and the sea. Because luckily there is the sea, to hide you, protect you, give you the courage to brave the wrath once again. Or advise you to wait till the nudists leave, at dusk, before coming out of your refuge.

III

THE NOVEL

I KNEW STRAIGHT AWAY THAT I wouldn't want to leave. The mountain was so round, it seemed to protect us, a huge breast capable of quenching the thirst of the entire little village. I would go home reluctantly, already looking forward to the following summer. Although I always travelled to the seaside with friends, I had been determined to come alone, completely alone, to this small inn nestled among the trees. The year had gone by so quickly, the seasons merging into one another so smoothly, that I woke up one morning staring with stupefaction at the blooming lilacs. I hadn't written a single line since the previous holidays.

Here, I would write, on the yellow balcony leading into the room that was painted yellow as well, which gave me the feeling I floated in mid-air. And that was exactly what I wanted: to float, to defy space, like kites one saw racing among the clouds at dusk. Absolute quiet, real silence, at long last what I called silence. There was no American music to hammer on our ears in the bars of big hotels, or near the swimming pool. None of the noise pollution that slowly ate away at us until we were numb. I was the only guest before the arrival of the woman in her mid-forties I had seen stepping out of a taxi the night before, her suitcase in her hand.

I could tell from the way she moved that she wouldn't bother me, and I went back to working on my novel. Even after all these months, the words stretched out on the page like cats that only needed to be stroked and they would give the sentences their sensuality. I smiled. Perhaps the woman had come to get over a recent heartache — my first reaction was always to think that people on their own were unhappy. But maybe she just wanted to forget about the din of the city. Or to write, like me.

In the morning, when I went into the dining room, she stood at the window that overlooked the rose garden. I only saw her from behind, her beautiful hair spilling over her shoulders, wearing a delicate, white, well-ironed blouse. I went to sit down by the other window, the one opening onto the verdant smell of the trees, with my back to her, so as not to be disturbed. But as soon as I heard the throaty voice of the proprietress, *So, Madame Barreiro, did you sleep well?* I turned around in spite of myself. It really was her, Maria Barreiro, I was sure of it, the woman who had refused to come to my brother's bedside. We had telephoned her twice. First my sister, then me. I had humbled myself, I had practically begged her. Jérémie had loved her deeply and only wanted one thing: to see her again for a few moments before he passed into the eternal silence. Maria Barreiro ordered coffee and croissants in that hoarse, cracked voice I had heard over the phone when she told me *No, I can't*, before hanging up.

I knew nothing, or next to nothing, about her affair with my brother. They had met on a trip. She had followed him. They lived together for two years. Then they parted. Jérémie never introduced her to the family. At Christmas, she used to go back to Valencia or stay with an uncle in New York. They shielded their love affair from us, and I didn't really mind — probably because I hoped the woman would vanish without a trace one day.

Jérémie finished his studies and met the man who was to remain by his side for the rest of his life. He was hired by a company in California. A wonderful career, as they say. He was happy until he was struck by the illness that entrenched itself in his kidneys and slowly spread, gnawing away at him bit by bit, consuming even the marrow of his bones. I shed rivers of tears. It couldn't be … my twin brother, the one who'd shared the narrow space of my mother's womb with me, who had kicked me and, later, pulled my ears and made fun of my breasts when I grew into a teenager, and then of my lovers. It was necessary to put a little distance between us. Since our childhood, Mama made every effort to separate us.

I struggled all morning with my novel, but wasn't able to add a single line. Since I'd heard the woman's name, the story I had started no longer interested me. Fiction was no match for reality. All I could think of was approaching Maria Barreiro, speaking to her, finding out why she had refused to see Jérémie again. With her lovely hair, the distinguished look about her, she didn't seem to be the type of woman who would meditate acts of revenge for decades, or to shirk from the last wishes of the dying. There had to be a motive. But even if she revealed it, how could I be sure she was telling the truth? And why this need to know the truth, as if my fate depended on it? It would take much more than Maria Barreiro's pathetic confession to rescue me from the depths of despair into which Jérémie's death had plunged me.

I left my characters to fend for themselves and walked to the village. Maria Barreiro sat at a table outside the only café, waiting for me, it seemed. She smiled at me and I sat down uninvited across from her. *I have followed you to this out-of-the-way inn*, she merely said. She had called my sister. She had pretended to be a colleague of mine. She hoped I wouldn't hold it against her, she added when I gave her a startled look. She was beautiful, better preserved than I, who had always taken lots of sunbaths, a ritual I never departed from, except last year. I would never have let Jérémie spend his final summer without me.

Tears now rolled down my cheeks. I had held such a grudge against this woman for taking my brother away from me. For the two years their affair lasted, I felt like an old object put away at the bottom of a drawer. That silent cry of joy when Jérémie told me they broke up! How I welcomed him when he came to take refuge in my home, how I put myself out, showing him I was there as I had always been before she, Maria Barreiro, turned up in his life.

She asked the waiter for two coffees, but with a steady voice I corrected her straight away, *A tea, an Earl Grey tea*. She wasn't going to make my decisions for me. We only drank tea in the family. She should know that, unless Jérémie began drinking coffee with her. There were so many things she knew about him and I didn't. I meant to ask her, *Tell me about Jérémie*, but I heard myself say, *Tell me about yourself*. Amused, Maria answered, *You will be disappointed*, but she complied. Perhaps to get the conversation going, she began describing her life in broad strokes: a happy childhood in Valencia, despite Franco, then she'd met my brother and wanted to live over here, even after the breakup. Now that Jérémie was gone, she had decided to go back to Spain. She added quickly, *Odd, isn't it: staying in a country because of a man one no longer sees?*

I discreetly lowered my eyes. As a matter of fact, I had never found out if it was because of Carlos that Jérémie and Maria broke up. My brother and I were always immensely guarded, a result of our religious upbringing, or of reticence within the family, or perhaps we just didn't want to talk about something that would always remain forbidden between us. By then, there had been men who had left me, but never for another man. I tried to imagine the feeling. Pain, as well as relief, to know that it wasn't for another woman. You would be powerless, utterly powerless. All you could do was resign yourself to what couldn't be changed.

Maria had a knack for reading people's minds. She began to talk about Carlos. She hadn't protested when he won Jérémie's affection. All was lost anyway, right from the beginning. She had to face the facts, she explained, looking me straight in the eye: there was only room for one woman in Jérémie's life, and that place was already taken, and had been from the moment he was conceived. How could she possibly intrude into a relationship begun in the dark waters of a womb? I didn't retort. I didn't say that when she, Maria, arrived, a rift had formed between Jérémie and me. She had split us up for good. It was thanks to her that both of us, on our own, could love someone, travel, live, and die, when our time came, without dragging the other along into nothingness.

I began, instead, to describe the novel I was writing, a story about exile. A man has been driven from his country and finds this extremely painful at first. All he thinks about are those he has left behind, mixing up in his dreams his mother, his brothers and sisters, his dog, and the sun. Then, following a revolution, he can go back, and he finds everything as it was: his family, his dog, the sun, the tropical vegetation. But he begins to dream of winters of ice and snow, and returns to the country that had welcomed him. Maria pensively turned her coffee cup around and around in her hands while I heard Carlos's story again, the one he told me during all those hours he and I watched over Jérémie at the hospital. Maria said she moved away from her country of her own free will, but was now ready to make peace with her childhood.

As for me, I never left the landscapes of my earliest years. A lack of imagination, or simply life's circumstances? A bit of all these things, probably. Yet I had travelled, discovered countries whose alphabets I was unable to decipher. I had crossed the sea and a few deserts, but I never lived in totally unfamiliar surroundings, not long enough, at least, to feel that a different woman might emerge in me. As an excuse — or to cheer myself up — I kept telling myself that it was in my writing that I became a different woman. And my friends and I often quoted Rimbaud: *I is someone else*. It was easier than leaving everything behind to go and tramp about in Abyssinia. Jérémie was no explorer either, but he had moved to California, the land of information technology. We knew nothing yet about Jérémie's private life. Even to me, he hadn't said anything. He waited for my first visit in California to introduce me to Carlos.

Everything had been said. Just by being there, Maria and I, enfolded in the mountain's shade, felt Jérémie's presence — a fair-haired ghost, a warm breeze, a spiritual body looking at us, with his emaciated features, and we submitted to his gaze. I let him look at me, sidelong at first, then more and more directly, and finally we looked into each other's eyes. I gradually slipped into a strange state, as if between the life of the living and that of the dead there existed only a porous boundary, a frontier incapable of separating us. I, who had fought so hard to keep Jérémie in this world for a few more days, was now being drawn into Jérémie's world, and this brought me peace. I had survived him, but he forgave me. He came to meet me, here, in this village, on this tranquil morning.

When I opened my eyes again, tears shone on Maria's face, and I liked to think that she, too, had briefly experienced another reality. In the midday brilliance, the mountain seemed to soar into space, as though to make us feel insignificant. Maria had to go and pack. She invited me to come and visit her in Spain. I promised, knowing full well we would never see each other again, but that was irrelevant. As irrelevant as finding out why she had been so anxious to see me.

I watched her slowly walk away, limping slightly. I felt a pang in my chest. Jérémie had never mentioned this. The waiter came up to me with the menu. I waved it aside and ordered a beer. Then I took my notebook and pen out of my bag. I had a strong sense that if I didn't immediately start working on my novel again, it would remain at the stage where it was — a heap of rough, craggy sentences, a pile of scattered sheets, a manuscript forever uncompleted.

TRAVELLING BACK

THAT'S THE WAY IT IS. Suddenly, the woman you have called Mother all your life is only a grey speck that looks for you but doesn't see you, over there, on the platform, her left hand shielding her eyes from the sun. You know she will stay there, until the last glance, the last wave, blinded by the glittering light, just barely able to make you out behind the dirty windows of the bus that will take you back to your own world. Yes, that's the way it is, you will say a little later to your husband, a glass of wine in your hand, almost casually. But a brief silence is all it takes for your sadness to well up again, and you will be just a little girl who cannot accept seeing her mother grow old.

In that other world, ambulance sirens pierced the air in summer nights when the windows were open. The harrowing whine of sirens. And it seems to you that all your memories come together in that long wail linked to the massive form of the hospital nearby, up on the hill, next to the house where Jovette Bernier had lived, the woman writer your mother sometimes spoke to you about. You already knew you wanted to write, too. But you hadn't discovered yet how much weight words could carry. You would say *Mama* or *my mother*, more neutral, more convenient — you hate to show emotion. You have never been able to say *Aline*. It would have felt like entering a forbidden room, the one where your mother undressed before your father's silent eyes.

There are moments in her life you don't want to imagine. The moment when the body surrenders to pleasure, or the skin tearing under the pressure from a child, or her ice-cold body laid out under the pale lights of a flower-filled room. You know you deny her the right to die. You don't notice her voice faltering now and then. You laugh tenderly when she talks about her neck getting more and more wrinkled. You point out the rosy flush on her cheeks when she excitedly tells you about the life of Proust she just finished. You aren't lying: you would love to have such a young-looking face when you're as old as she is. She will live to a great age, like Eugénie, her grandmother. And so will you. You'll write until you are ninety-five. You swear you will.

Your own skin is still intact, or almost. There are a few lines at the corners of your eyes, so, to cheer yourself up, you say *intact*. Like the river flowing sluggishly in its bed through rustling foliage. One doesn't smell the industrial waste or the oil patches floating on top of the water, a greasy soup, a poor-people's soup. But that must have been in earlier days. The river has become pristine again, your mother tells you, but you don't believe her. You never make this journey with the eyes of who you are now. You strain to recognize every tree, every street, and every church in this town you have never completely left.

Some day, you won't come back. Your childhood will be buried in the flowery little graveyard. Perhaps you'll drop by once in a while, with one of your daughters, to lay a small bouquet at the foot of the headstone. But you don't dwell on that thought. You leave it hovering at the far end of the sky, at some distant point on the horizon. That time hasn't come yet. The bus is about to turn into the access road leading to the highway. The town is behind you. You hunt for the magazine you bought for the trip. Here it is. You spot the cover of Proust's *Within a Budding Grove*. You smile. When your mother handed you the book, she said, *All those rich, carefree people. I would love to hear the maid's point of view*. Your mind drifts back to the clothes passed down by your cousins, to the piano lessons you couldn't take, to bringing only pennies to school for the church missions, to what they called budgeting at home. The word poverty was reserved for others, for the really poor, the little girls in school who didn't have a Sunday dress. You suddenly understand why you've waited so long before reading Proust.

Even so, there was happiness. Not the noun, which is too direct, too brazen. The happiness you heard about at home was more modest. The workaday kind, contained in the adjective happy. *You are a happy woman*. It was Théo Chentrier who said so on the radio in his patriarchal voice. He spoke to your mother. She had written to him. Every morning, at ten o'clock, he answered letters from listeners, and your mother's ear would be glued to the radio so she wouldn't miss a word. On school holidays, you listened, too, ensconced in the rocking chair, and you learnt about life. Husbands who didn't wash themselves. Rivalry between sisters-in-law. The nasty woman next door. Jealousy. For the first time, you saw your mother as a woman striving to be happy, with her husband and children, a woman who applied herself to the art of transforming ordinary things into splashes of light. *An art of living*, said Théo Chentrier, and your mother smiled. Then came, *I have loved you so much*, and you'd hear about happiness in capital letters, involving great passions and quivering voices. One day, you would be grown-up. You would no longer be entangled in your mother's happy life. You, too, would experience rapturous love affairs.

A patch of deep blue sky, an old barn, cows standing motionless in a field. You don't know which image beyond the window takes you back to your first trip to Montréal, with that boy who was going to be your lover. You wore black underwear, bought on sale, and nail polish. You practised bringing your cigarette to your lips with an elegant flourish, as in the theatre. You wanted a husband who wasn't like your father. A sophisticated man with beautiful manners, who could read and write fluently. At night, the two of you would discuss literature and the cinema, and then make love with ecstatic screams. You would be proud of him when you walked on his arm to your children's school to pick up their report cards.

It would take several years before you could distinguish between books and real life, and even longer to understand your mother's love for your father. Now you know. She did love him and expects you to love him, too. You want to tell her that you love him, of course, but not like a father. Like an uncle or a cousin you would have shared a house with, rather. Like someone too deprived to protect you. Yes, that's what you should tell your mother. And yet ... There are certain things about yourself you cannot confess to her.

ALL THE GARDENS, ALL THE PARKS

RIGHT THERE. WE WILL MEET again right there. On a bench. That's what she wants to imagine. He'll be reading a novel, an American bestseller, say the latest Paul Auster, and she'll go up to him, sit down beside him, on the same painted, wooden bench. She'll open a magazine, for appearances' sake, so she won't feel awkward while she waits to see. Yes, right there. When she has learnt to do without him, when she has become a woman again in whose life he plays no role, a woman no longer waiting.

She asked him to leave and he did. No shouts, no unfortunate gestures that shatter all lingering hope. A single sentence, *Please leave now*. He headed towards the door without looking back, and she would keep that image of him in her mind forever — his familiar walk ahead of her in the corridor before he vanished into the night. Her eyes followed him to his car. She knew it was over, the way people might say, it's over between us, without really believing it at first.

And then she is alone again, because everything has been said. But the slightest thing awakens memories: a certain movement, someone running his hand through his hair, a reminder of a city that rekindles desire, Rome or Athens, narrow streets where they strolled hand in hand, scenes of perfect happiness, two bodies in the languor of dusk. How much time will it take to forget? How long will it be before the heart becomes a hollow muscle again? She has come to a standstill, faced with grief she cannot put a name to. In the mirror, she has the eyes of survivors who have lost their souls under the debris. In spite of everything, she has survived. She will have to relearn how to eat, how to laugh, how to take pleasure in another man's gaze. She will just have to.

Almost July already. The days and the nights sink into a formless expanse of time. She is utterly still for hours on end, waiting for something she cannot define, perhaps the very thing she is no longer waiting for. She has to shake off her torpor then and get moving, put her feet on the ground so she won't turn to stone. In the nervous hum of the late afternoon, she walks until her legs stop carrying her. She forces her way through the motley crowd of people streaming out of offices. She will hide away in the park. She has her own bench, in front of the pond, the one where some day she will see him again. Will he look much older? she wonders. Will she have trouble recognizing him with wrinkles and grey hair? Will he still have that smooth, open smile?

Every day, she goes to the park, and every day, she sits on the bench. Hoping, for another state of grace, for the old smells, the old places. Yes, we'll meet again. Where is she when he sits down on the bench, right beside her, without her noticing? She barely turns her head when he points to the child at the edge of the pond, a fair-haired boy throwing pebbles at the ducklings just for fun. She opens her eyes wide, brought back to reality all of a sudden. *What a violent child*, she says. *We should do something*. But the duck has already moved her ducklings. Perturbed, the boy flings his last pebbles against the trunk of a maple tree and runs off.

He repeats, *What a violent child*. Then she really looks at him. His face, the features of his face, his rather thick lips, his straight nose. She examines him as though she hadn't seen a man for a very long time. It doesn't seem to surprise him. He lets her look at him and then breaks the silence, *You come every afternoon*. She turns her head away to protect herself. She only whispers, *I am learning to be alone* and hears him answer, *I know. You walk as though you still adjust your pace to someone else's*. In her mind, she sees him heading down the corridor, going through the door for the last time, descending the steps to his car.

She must look preoccupied, because he repeats, *As though you still adjust your pace to someone else's*. There is something disconcerting about the phrase: she pictures herself trotting along behind a shadow and she smiles. She smiles at him. Gently he moves closer, slips his arm around her shoulders and ventures some trivial remark about the sultriness in the air, the storm that is about to break. She nods. Yes, the storm. Perhaps they will get caught in it while they're in the park.

Does it really matter? But he tells her they should leave, and she finds herself standing next to a man who leads her towards the street.

For how long do they walk without saying a word? She couldn't say exactly. He has taken her arm and she follows him listlessly. She neither agrees nor refuses when he suggests they have dinner in a small café whose owner he knows very well. She sees herself stepping into a room with too much lighting, being shown to a seat by the waiter, without understanding what is happening to her. She smiled at this man and now she will eat with him, as if he were that other man. She thinks of all the meals they shared in restaurants like this one, the laughter, the heart-to-heart talks, what is called a story, as in books. Yes, the closeness, the laughter, the plans, more laughter, and lovemaking after they'd had a bit too much to drink, the evening ending very late in a crumpled bed.

She bends her head, tries to concentrate on the menu, and gives her order in a voice meant to be steady. He asks her if she will have a glass of wine and, out of bravado, she nods. Why not? She can leave her grief in a tiny recess of her heart, long enough to have dinner, long enough to make herself think she is still alive, can't she? He offers her some bread and she notices he has nice hands — broad fingers with neatly trimmed nails. She blushes. As if she didn't have the right to look, not yet. He talks to her. He is a good conversationalist. Now he asks her questions about her occupation. She hears herself answer, *Freelance journalist*, and he is satisfied with this.

She doesn't need to go into details: gleaning contracts here and there for decorating magazines, the difficulty to make ends meet certain months, like this one, when she hasn't been able to get through the usual amount of work.

How about him? *I am a sculptor*, he replies. The word holds her attention. She looks at his hands again, the hands of a sculptor. For a second, she wonders how such fingers caress a woman's body. She chases the image away and tries to take an interest in his explanations, but only catches isolated words, *metal*, *marble*, *ebony*, *installation*. She nods in agreement, yet before long she will have to utter a sentence. How will she manage it? But he already moves on to the holidays. He has a place in the country. He'll be leaving soon, in two or three weeks. Does she have any travel plans? She could come and stay with him for a few days. There is a stream, there are mountains, she would return to Montréal completely refreshed. He makes her promise she'll come. She promises, but doesn't feel committed. She may very well change her mind at the last minute. In a couple of hours, he himself will probably have forgotten. What does she know about him, after all? She can't even remember his first name. Besides, she hasn't asked him for anything. He sought her out on her bench, in the park, on a stormy evening.

It's raining heavily now, and suddenly she feels more at ease. Across from her, he fills the silence as if he fears their encounter is so fragile it may disappear into thin air. Does she like him? She can't tell. And yet it seems to her that something quite obscure within her has already answered yes. She feels she would let that man undress her. She wants to run away, head for the door, disappear in the gathering darkness. But she stays, listening, nodding slowly, until the sentence, *Do you always agree like that?* His tone has turned impatient, she disappoints him. At the bottom of her glass, she spots her blurred image. She struggles to her feet, picks up her bag, and leaves. Flashes of lightning rip through the city. In a few seconds she will be soaking wet. Already her clothes cling to her skin, but she will walk all the way home rather than hail a taxi, so she won't be forced to hold back her tears. She will walk through the streets alone.

She feels a hand brushing against her arm and utters a cry. Then she calms down and simply says, *You frightened me very much*. She hadn't heard him coming. He apologizes. *I was very frightened myself. Of losing you*. He lives three minutes away from there. He invites her over to his place. They have so much to say to each other. She doesn't understand what makes her accept. Perhaps his tone of voice, his sincerity, that admission. How can he have been afraid of losing her while she wanders about on a devastated planet, lost already to herself? He takes her to a place with huge windows. *For the light*, he explains, while he shows her his latest sculptures. She looks at them, but doesn't dare go near them, confused by this world she hadn't suspected, this baffling, foreign world she is trying to get used to — metal and acute angles capturing space in bold, uncompromising forms.

He holds a robe out to her, a large one, one of his. She goes to take off her clothes in the bathroom. When she comes back, he starts to laugh. *You look as if you had been shipwrecked.* She bursts out laughing, too. Her tenseness has gone. She can trust him. He doesn't want to be sharp with her. Now he is making tea — *very hot tea*, he stresses — and asks her to pick the music. She takes a Philip Glass album out of its case. The room becomes inhabited. She'll be able to talk. And she will.

They talk about all sorts of things, the small details that anchor one's life: home renovations, how to organize one's time when one does freelance work, the latest movie hits. He makes more tea, and still more tea, until the first light of dawn comes through the plant-filled window. She talks as in the days before everything changed. She remembers and slips into that old self, simply because this man is there.

Already a hum rises from the city. Soon, it will be daylight. But she is too exhausted to go home. She is the one who asks if she may lie down on the sofa. He offers his bed. They can sleep chastely side by side, can't they? She has nothing to fear. She lets him take her to the bedroom. No sooner has she noticed the abstract pattern on the sheets than she drifts off to sleep — a bottomless, dreamless, untroubled sleep. When she awakes, she doesn't know what time it is, but the sun is already high up in the sky. She recalls she has slept beside a stranger and doesn't dare turn her head. But he is up already, so she will have time to get her bearings.

On the bedside table, right beside her, she spots the title

of Paul Auster's new novel, and is amused by the coincidence. Strangely enough, she doesn't feel overwhelmed by her grief. The day looks almost joyful. And now he comes back carrying a tray with coffee, croissants, and jam. He is smiling. Fabulous weather. Would she agree to spend the day with him? They'll go for a walk, they could return to the park if she wants, feed the ducks, have a bite to eat on a terrace. There is so much for them to do. He doesn't feel like seeing her go.

He uttered that last sentence almost shyly. The only possible answer is, *I have been deeply hurt*, but he comes up to her in the warm fragrance of the coffee and she lets him stroke the nape of her neck, and her back, while slowly, discreetly, he takes off her robe. She hides her face in her hands, and then turns towards him, the way one forces oneself when one has made certain decisions. There has to be a first time, for feeling the breath of another man in her neck, other lips on her breasts, so why not this morning? She offers herself. She will watch him take her without being able to utter a word. She will have to submit, silently submit at every moment, say yes to the ritual.

When he puts his hand on her thigh, he notices the tears she is trying to hold back. He slides onto his side and presses himself against her shoulder while he ventures, *You don't look like a woman who's ready to let the archangels sing*. She gives the ghost of a smile, then laughs faintly through her tears, but laughs nevertheless. He said the right thing. He lies very close to her, stroking her hair, and she confesses in a broken voice, *You'll have to be patient with me*. She hears him murmur, *Does Madam want me to get out the chessboard?* He kisses her ear. What would she rather do: first coffee and croissants and then go for a walk? Or go and sit on the bench in the park together?

She shakes her head. Not the park today. They can find somewhere else to go, the Jardin botanique, the Vieux-Port, or a spot where she has never been. She is no longer worried. She seeks his gaze. A patch of light flickers across the dimple in his right cheek. He suddenly looks like a schoolboy. Slowly she runs her finger over his face, as if to get to know it, make sure she will recognize it, and murmurs, *Do you think the coffee can wait?* What makes her say this? Tenderly, he draws her down. *The coffee*, he replies, *the Vieux-Port, and all the gardens, all the parks in the world*. He kisses her. She lets herself be kissed. She goes along with it. Soon, he will penetrate into her secret place, find his way inside her. In the deepest reaches of her body, she will feel the slow coming of the first, wrenching, break.

THE BROOCH

For Werner Nold

THE ROOM WAS PACKED. WELL-DRESSED people, beautifully coiffed, refined — or trying to be, at least. Although we were in the middle of May, it was stiflingly hot. Why on earth had I come to this party? But twenty-five years for a publishing house, in such a small country, surely merited the trip. I kept telling myself that one mustn't forget, one must be grateful, when I spotted her near the table where the wine was being served. Red hair, black dress, an ever-present piece of silver jewellery pinned above her left breast, just as pretty as before she left for the United States, twenty years or so earlier. She recognized me instantly, and I threaded my way through the clusters of visitors that were forming. People laughed, whooped, kissed. What a wonderful opportunity to meet again, here, after all those years! She opened her arms to hug me, but I froze, mesmerized by her brooch, a solid-silver pear. My pear, the one that had been stolen in a burglary of my home in mid-March. A friend had crafted it for me after taking courses in jewellery-making. *A pear with walnut leaves*, he pointed out when he gave it to me for my birthday.

I blamed the unbearable heat when she asked me if I was all right, and she added, *The menopause*? I agreed. I would have agreed with anything in order to give myself time to collect my wits. It certainly hadn't been Marie-Claire, after all, who had broken into my home on that Sunday afternoon when I had gone to a concert. The outrage I had felt at dusk when I came back to an apartment that resembled a battlefield! Drawers, wardrobes, filing cabinet! *The job was done by professionals*, the police said confidently. The burglars had taken my passport, my credit cards, my laptop, and my jewellery. All my jewellery. No diamonds or precious stones, no, just souvenirs, things I'd bought on my travels over the years, trinkets found in flea markets, and Christmas or birthday presents, like that pear, which I prized above all else. I had wept with sadness and anger, and then I'd calmed down, but the scene came back to me now, along with the sadness and the anger. I was like a boiling volcano.

I don't know how I managed to keep a grip on myself. Apparently, I did. With perfect composure, I watched the pear jump up and down on Marie-Claire's ample bosom, while she told me in painstaking detail about her eventful life in Washington. All along, I responded to her story with gestures, facial expressions, monosyllables, while searching for a phrase that would let me move smoothly to the topic of her pretty silver brooch: she had always had such wonderful taste! But suddenly there was a loud shriek. My face must have dropped. Odile fell into our arms — not at all surprising, though, since people had come here to see each other again. Then Solange turned up, with her auburn curls, and that handsome Paul-André. If my memory served me right, he had had an affair with Marie-Claire. Yes, I was sure. I could tell from the way they looked at one another — deep into each other's eyes, the place from which images emerged that lovers thought they had forgotten.

I decided to go home. I didn't have the patience to wait for miracles anymore. Goodbyes and kisses. *Let's make a point of getting together soon*, said Marie-Claire. I quickly slipped my card into her hand and airily walked through the door. A cool breeze. It wasn't quite so suffocating. I decided to walk home. A stroll would give me a chance to sort things out in my mind. Seeing my brooch on Marie-Claire's breast had triggered a bout of nostalgia. However hard I tried not to dwell on the past, a whole chapter of my life resurfaced nonetheless. Hopes, love affairs, friendships, convictions. Marie-Claire and I had been activists together. I had had my son only a few weeks after the birth of her daughter, Émilie, an adorable little girl until she fell in love with a drug dealer in high school. The usual story. Marie-Claire had been mad with worry. She was on the verge of despair when she was offered the job in Seattle, a real godsend. Her daughter hadn't even grumbled about moving to the West Coast, as if she were glad she finally had a good reason for leaving her boyfriend. Émilie was back in Montréal, too. This was all Marie-Claire had time to tell me — I would find out more when we'd meet again. She would call me. I was sure she would. In fact, she left a message for me that same evening. She suggested we have lunch at the café where she and I used to go in the past and have our great talks.

The following day, the sun blazed down on the city again as if it were July. Restaurant terraces swarmed with people. Inside the café, there was no one. I sat down at a quiet table near the window and glanced at passersby. Marie-Claire was late, as in the old days. There she was now with her sunglasses. She got out of a Jaguar convertible and turned around to blow a kiss to the driver — black slicked-back hair, early forties, the type I had always found insufferable, somewhere between a well-off young man from a wealthy family and a mobster boss. The complete opposite of Paul-André. But the occasional contradiction had never bothered Marie-Claire, not even in our uncompromising years, which had endeared her to me, although many activists had been suspicious of her.

Still in a state of shock, I didn't notice her bare blouse when she sat down across from me. Not for a moment did I think of my brooch, left at the bottom of a drawer or on top of a dresser. All I was interested in was her new flame. She hadn't mentioned him to me at the party. True, it hadn't been the ideal spot to tell of one's conquests. As casually as I could, I said, *You look wonderful. You seem to be in great shape.* But the waitress interrupted us right away. Were we ready to order? We pored over the day's menu so we could carry on with our talk as quickly as possible. After all, we had arranged to meet so we could renew our friendship. Twenty years ... We would have been able to spend whole days together, telling each other about the best and the worst. How could we have lost touch for so long? My efforts to steer the conversation towards the man with the Jaguar failed utterly. It was as though he didn't exist for Marie-Claire. I practised patience while hurriedly telling her how my son was doing. Yes, Philippe had just finished his master's. He had an insecure job right now. His situation was similar to that of other young people his age. He continued to move through life in a straight line. Like mother like son, it would appear. *I have never been as bold as you*, I said emphatically. Marie-Claire laughed but didn't rise to the bait. Her eyes shining with emotion, she murmured, *Remember when we used to take the children to La Ronde?*

Then the frames of a film, of which we knew every scene, flashed past our eyes: the excitement of Philippe and Émilie, their little faces covered with candy floss, my dizzy spell on the Ferris wheel, the trip home at night on the metro when we were totally exhausted. A pang in my chest. So many years already. Our children were now the age we were then. I, too, had a sip of wine without adding another word. Marie-Claire drank to our health. She shared my loathing for hackneyed phrases about time robbing us all.

To come back to the present, I asked after Émilie. My old friend's face lit up again. Her daughter was unquestionably the great love of her life. Once Marie-Claire started talking about her, she could go on forever. She went over everything, right from the moment they left for Seattle: high school, university, Émilie's good marks, good conduct, good manners, the good company she kept. I listened to her with only half an ear, but touched nonetheless by her story. A mother was a mother was a mother, no doubt about it. We weren't any different from the women who came before us, no matter how critical we were of them and of ourselves.

The coffee had arrived and I still hadn't asked a single question about my brooch. I did have to get to it, though, while Marie-Claire told me about her daughter's great love. *Émilie is married*, she said. She paused for effect and then added, *She married well, by the way*. A businessman she met on a plane. He travelled a lot, import-export. Actually, he was the one who had driven her here, in a Jaguar no less. She would have introduced him to me if he hadn't had an urgent appointment. I drained my wine to hide a fit of helpless laughter, while Marie-Claire continued her praise. Dave was so thoughtful — he had given her a silver brooch for Mother's Day. The pear she wore yesterday? Yes, the very one — the one I seemed to like. That pear was one of a kind, Marie-Claire explained, and I managed to ask if this Dave had found it in Montréal. Marie-Claire didn't know — her son-in-law had so many contacts and was involved in so many lines of business, and he spent a lot of time abroad. That was her only motherly worry, that Émilie might feel lonely now and then, when she had her baby. Émilie, a child with him?

She stopped, delighted by my astonishment. She had really succeeded in surprising me.

At the next table, the woman looked at me. I must have shouted almost. Marie-Claire thought it was from emotion, or envy. I, too, would have the great joy of being a grandmother some day. She hoped I would. Philippe was sure to meet a young woman who'd be as fine a person as Dave. An odd, uneasy feeling crept over me. How could Marie-Claire be so naive! And yet I kept quiet. Out of fondness for her, or a lack of courage? I didn't know. I opened my bag to take out my wallet. My fingers brushed against the photo of my pear. I had brought it along to prove to her that the pear was mine, but it would stay hidden in my bag. I cleared my throat to say firmly, *This is my treat, Marie-Claire. I insist. This is my treat.*

A BOTTLE IN THE SEA

EYES CLOSED, YOU GO FORWARD in darkness. You don't know where the road will take you. Since your mother died, you have walked a lightless path. Your mother is dead, you say, but she is still very much alive. You say it to get used to it, so you will be able to say it when the time comes. A betrayal perhaps, but you say it anyway. Your mother has died. You hope her death will be like her own mother's. Quick and peaceful.

On an afternoon like any other, her bowels had suddenly emptied. She called. She was ashamed of having soiled her white sheets, and then she died, in the disgrace of a fouled bed. Your mother was there. So were you. Only the three of you. Your grandmother, ashamed of her bowels emptying, your mother, and you. *The bowels, just before the end*, your mother whispered. That's what you remember of her death: the body doing its job one last time. You didn't see your own death. Teenagers cannot see that.

The deaths of the women of your flesh and blood are neither heroic nor desperate. These women don't go to war or kill themselves. Their deaths are so ordinary you almost shrink from describing them. Quiet, like their lives. The years succeeding one another, children, daily meals, sewing clothes by lamplight, and, later, grandchildren. Then, one day, the thread breaks. One hadn't noticed it was slowly fraying. Blindly — that is perhaps how one should go forward. You do.

But you exaggerate. Your mother's eyes are open. She is often afraid. Afraid of taking forever to die, of lingering on, more dead than alive. There is no way of knowing how one will end. She admits this in a whisper, late at night, when time stands still in the building where she lives, and you grope for reassuring words, but you don't find them. So you keep silent. You listen.

You keep silent. You always have, with her. Try as you might to sit up straight in your chair, to open your mouth, the words stick together in your throat, choke you sometimes, and all you can do is repeat trite phrases. With your mother, you are still the schoolgirl who brought home excellent report cards at the end of the month to see her smile. You were the perfect little girl, and you go back to that role whenever you visit her. Your sisters, too. She may not have had an easy life, but she will have had good children.

She will have been what is called a good mother. Love, care, and attention, a happy environment, help with your homework. She read you bedtime stories and, on rainy autumn Sundays, she would gently slide reproductions of paintings out of their protective sleeves. She taught you the names of Renoir, Cézanne, Degas, and Monet well before your high-school days. You are grateful. You can say it now without bitterness. It's not because you have never been able to talk with her that you cannot value her.

You tried. You did try to talk, to tell her what sort of woman you have become with the passing years. But you hit against a wall of silence. One day, it occurred to you that, ensconced in her orderly life, your mother couldn't hear you — you with your emotional outpourings. She was afraid of you, as she was now afraid of death. Of course, you had to accept it in the end, but you still dream that your mother talks to you as to a woman. You sit down across from her, she looks at you with a smile, she asks, *How are you?* And you start talking to her in a genuine voice. But you soon snap back to reality.

Little by little, you faced the facts. One cannot change anyone, least of all one's mother. You remember at what precise moment you gave up. One snowy morning, you decided to talk to her about your aunt. To put the past into words, you used the word *mad*. But your mother denied it at once. She went back to her old topics: the house, the neighbours, the shopping for the week. Yet she had heard you perfectly well. Of that, you are absolutely sure. But she refused to open the breach you spotted in her eyes for a fraction of a second.

You say *breach*, but does the word really cover what she had managed to hide from you until then? Since it happened — this you know — there has been a blind spot, a hole in the middle of her life, an abyss threatening to swallow her up whenever she goes near the edge. So she skirts it, fences it in. She does every single thing the way it should be done. She says, *One shouldn't pay too much attention to one's feelings*. She will have spent her life not paying attention to her feelings.

But how would *you* have acted if one of your sisters had gone mad one day without anyone knowing how to treat her? Psychiatrists, electric shock therapy, drugs, and your grandparents no longer able to look after your aunt — you remember those hushed conversations when you were a child. You remember being on your best behaviour while you wondered if you, too, would be sent to a mental hospital some day. And the consuming fear that made the blood rush to your temples.

Fear. Yes, fear is what the past continually brings back to you. As it does to your mother, no doubt. She will have made her way through life by carefully putting one foot in front of the other so as not to fall. You wish she had taught you how to run or to waltz, but you took your first dance steps alone. When you were younger, you resented that — don't deny it — even at times when you still held out hope. You imagined the two of you walking arm in arm. You were going to a restaurant or the theatre. With her, you savoured the pleasure of heart-to-heart talks. One day, you noticed she had grown old, and you gave up. You went back to your role of loving daughter.

Between you and her, there have been no words, but lots of acts. Jars of jam in the fall, knitted socks in winter, blouses mended by the window. One can love, and yet not be able to talk. Your mother loves you. She does. She loves you as a little girl, but not as the woman she can no longer protect. That woman has grown away from her. Your mother wants to know neither her strength nor her anxieties. So she draws the red-haired little girl with russet eyes towards her into a bubble that burst a long time ago, and tells you stories she has told you a hundred times before. To mask your boredom, you listen for the slightest word that might be hidden beneath the spoken ones, the word that would reveal your mother's enigma.

Some day, her body will empty itself for the last time. You hope you will be there, by her side, as she was with her mother. You will clean her. You will do what she did every day before you learnt to talk. You will say to your daughter, *Just before the end, the bowels*, thinking of your own death. How will you react? That question sometimes slips into your mind when you leave her building. You have resigned yourself to her muteness — you believe so, anyway — but just as she closes her eyes, you may feel tremendous regret. The familiar body, which you'll cover with a white sheet, will have kept its mystery until the end. You will blame yourself for having been unable to get her to confide in you.

Is that why you write, like those women whose books you gently open at night, at bedtime? Silent, like you, when they face their mothers — that is how you picture them. Some come from countries you have travelled to, others from regions where you will never go. But they are there, very close, under the lamp. They send you their words full of anger, compassion, or happiness sometimes. They trust you. They are sure you will welcome them.

The glorious miracle of books: a bottle tossed into the sea, which another woman will pick up some day. You hope so, at least. You will have found the words she hadn't learnt to say. Her heart will begin to beat again. She will take her pen and scribble page after page, but probably you will never find out, because you will never know her.

EVENING'S END

AFTERWARDS, THE TABLECLOTH REMINDS YOU of a plundered town. Gravy rings overlapping wine stains, torn bread crusts, glasses edged with red lips. You remember the mouths stretching open, earlier, to gobble up the meats, the mechanical motions of the jaws. And yet, perfect graciousness, refinement, restraint by bodies that have left the gluttony of childhood behind. It surprises you that, despite everyone's good manners, chaos re-emerged. A brief spell of oblivion, of indulgence in the pleasure of simple things.

Alone now, you clear the table. You tidy up. You make repeated trips back and forth between the dining room and the kitchen. You rinse. You wash. You throw an admiring glance at the old china's delicate flowers, as you did when you where a little girl while putting the tiny set of dishes, inherited from a great-aunt, back in its box.

At each visit from your cousins, you laid the small table — pink tablecloth, plastic cutlery made to look like silverware, plates, cups and saucers. You would go to the kitchen to get biscuits and warm water faintly flavoured with tea, which you enjoyed while chattering away. That was called playing.

You don't see the cousins anymore. They are married women, with children. All you happened to hear was that Sylvie suffered from depression. *I can't figure it out*, her mother had said. *Such a beautiful home. What more can anyone want?* You hadn't answered. You had thought of calling her, but what was the use of sitting across from one another like strangers?

Around the table, a little while ago, there was laughter, there were stories, memories. The Czech Republic, Switzerland, Finland, Québec, too, the Québec of the fifties. You felt the need to anchor the present in the past. You forged a bond among yourselves. Hadn't you said goodbye to the early seasons of your lives to be here, together, alive, vibrantly alive? Was it Maria or Karina who proposed a toast to friendship? It doesn't matter. You can still see the glasses clinking above the candle flames. You still feel moved by the sweetness of that moment. A miracle. You hope this small gesture can ward off ill fortune.

On the faces, the years have slowly entrenched themselves in the flesh. More and more often, you think of the wrinkled skin of your mother. *Two years since I saw her*, Eva murmurs, choking back a sob. You are used to living without looking back, dry-eyed. You accept the consequences of your choices. You face up to reality. Yet, sometimes, in the middle of a conversation, nostalgia will resurface, and you feel yourself weakening — the fragrant air of May, cloudless skies, a lilac branch picked on the way home from school, a furtive kiss stolen behind a tree, love ruled by chance.

The house is neat again. You should go to bed, but you aren't sleepy. You want to sink into a warm bubble bath to draw the evening out a little more, to fix in a deep recess of your memory these reassuring words, *We will never lose touch*. You seek certainties — at this blessed hour, at least, when all it takes are a few illusions to mask the dismal darkness of the night.

THE LAST OCTOBER

THIS WILL BE THE LAST time she'll go into the building. The last time she'll enter the access code to open the door. She will take the elevator to the fourth floor. He will let her in, help her out of her coat. Then they'll chat. What will she talk about with him? What does one talk about with a man who no longer resembles himself? His face puffed up, his head bald from the treatments, looking like an old man — she hardly recognized him when she saw him again, at the beginning of the week. She knew, but reality only registers on us through the eyes. *The die is cast*, he confessed to her in a voice that was grave but still firm. A matter of snatching another week, another month from life, the way one digs a shelter in time. He cried. She had never seen him shed a tear before. She wiped his cheek, and, calmed, he smiled at her.

When she met him, how old was he? The age she is now. But she thought he was already old, she recalls. Even boys in their twenties seemed on the verge of retirement to her. She laughs about it with her friends. Her students are flabbergasted that she has a son their age. She makes no secret of it. What's the use? They'll remember as they approach fifty, the time when one starts to draw up the balance sheet. Credit, debit. Can a brilliant career make us forget about the years that are sucked, one after the other, into a bottomless pit?

Autumnal light shines on the city this morning. Café terraces are deserted. The tourists have gone home. When she was younger, she would have liked to live in this city, which, through her travels, has become more and more familiar to her. She had felt a twinge of sorrow when he told her he was leaving. What luck! He was offered a position in his country. He would end his career there. When he retired, he would go back to his native town, where the archives he needed were kept. He would be able to carry on with his research in perfect happiness. He still had so much to do. Sad to be losing him, her mentor, she had done her best to smile. She had also felt envy. He painted a picture of a dream life in a dream city, whereas she had spent her holidays preparing her courses for the next term. But he had been through that, too. Lectures, work to correct, administrative duties. And she, too, would regain her freedom one day.

She wouldn't trade professions with anyone, though. The students. The exchanges with specialists. This conference, for example, an unexpected opportunity to come back here, to see him again, before it was too late. These past months, while reading the letters he'd written her with a trembling hand, she had chosen not to understand how much havoc the illness was wreaking. Just as she had never understood death, not even in funeral parlours, surrounded by carnations. As though a mere request, a plea, a gesture might bring the sleeping person back to the land of the living. A remnant from her childhood, perhaps. She had been told so many stories at school about people rising from the dead. She had stopped believing in miracles ages ago, and yet …

He had begun complaining about headaches at the beginning of the summer, but he wasn't worried. He had been working too hard, not getting enough sleep. The doctor advised him to rest. She had stressed her point. Why such a mad pace? Did the fact of having crammed in one more lecture make any difference when one breathed one's last? But she was stating her own logic, while he piled up presentations the way financiers accumulated shares. He felt obscurely that his end was near. Why hadn't she understood?

The boulevard, now. Noise from motorbikes, the smell of gasoline so typical of cities hewn out of the rock. The building. The building where he is waiting for her. He is alone. They still leave him alone, but for how much longer? What will happen in the coming months? She doesn't know, or, rather, she does. Memory gradually growing dim, the body declining. Death throes. This morning, he talks about it quite calmly, like a man who can read the future. *You think you will live forever*, he had said to her a few years ago, when she added more and more health foods to her diet. She had laughed. But since then, she'd had the chance to notice how radically, in North America, the signs of the passage of time are denied. Old buildings, monasteries, everything can be razed. Erased. Even bodies can be renovated, with money. Youth, like a religion.

He is no more a believer than she is. Yet, they have visited historic churches together. She asked him one day to take her to a synagogue. She had tiptoed in, followed his hushed explanations. Then they'd stepped out and vanished into the dazzling August sunshine. He is not a believer but, this morning, she's almost tempted to ask him if, at the time when we draw up our accounts with life, childhood catches up with us, and the name of God.

So many questions crowd into her mind, yet she won't ask them. It isn't reticence, but rather a numbness she feels in all her limbs, while she listens, sitting across from him, in this colourful living room. He talks and she listens. She tries to absorb all his sentences, as at the lectures he used to give at university. What has stayed with her from that time? She has forgotten almost everything he taught, but she has kept her passion for literature. It was his most precious gift to her, which she strives, in turn, to pass on to her students. Does he know? She should try to tell him. She won't be there to close his eyes. She will get a long-distance call, one fine day, a few weeks from now or a few months. It is impossible to tell how long a body can hold out before it agrees to let go. But the man opposite her is still very much alive. He actually wants to go for a walk now.

The weight of his heavy form clinging to her arm, her fear he'll have one of his weak spells, the surprised looks from passersby — she will remember it all. She wants to. She edges forward, engraves every sound, every image on her mind, while she wonders how she'll feel the first time she'll take this walk alone. There will be other trips, other autumns resembling bleak summers, splashes of light striking the ground. For now, he steps along through pools of sunshine. He talks, quite freely. He gets angry with motorists. He laughs. Perhaps he has forgotten he will not see next year's October. And she strolls along beside him, supporting him. She smiles. Wanting to have him believe, for the space of a walk, in the immortality of the present, in the everlasting caress of the wind on his skin. Wanting to protect this moment.

But they must go back. They will walk down the boulevard together, take the elevator to the apartment. She will sit with him for a little while longer, and then get up. She will need to force herself to get up, leave him there, among his books. With a lump in her throat, she will turn around to smile at him, one more time. She won't notice the death mask stamped on his face. She won't go to the museum or the movies. She will spend the afternoon wandering through the city. Ahead of her, a face will slowly loom out of the distance. The face of a woman who, one day, will welcome for the last time a former student.

BIBLIOGRAPHICAL NOTE

Some of the stories in this collection were originally published in somewhat different forms in the following:

Arcade (Montréal): "Pas à pas" ("Step by Step"), under the title "Funambule," no. 54, 2002; "Les yeux givrés" ("Snow-covered Eyes"), under the title "Les yeux gelés," no. 25, 1992; "L'Étoile" ("The Star"), no. 31, 1994; "Le retour" ("Travelling Back"), no. 45, 1999; "Fin de soirée" ("Evening's End"), no. 27, 1993; "Le dernier octobre" ("The Last October"), no. 62, 2004.

Catalogue of *Artefact Montréal 2007: Sculptures urbaines / Urban Sculptures*, (on the theme of Expo 67): "Babel heureuse" ("A Happy Babel"), Centre d'art public, 2008.

Un lac, un fjord, un fleuve: Jardins secrets (Les Éditions JCL, Chicoutimi): "Le dé à coudre" ("The Thimble"), 1991.

VWA (Switzerland): "Le monde vidé" ("A Vacant World"), no. 26, 1998–1999.

Moebius (Montréal): "Histoire de poupée" ("Doll Story"), no. 47, 1991.

XYZ. La revue de la nouvelle (Montréal): "Un rire" ("A Certain Laugh"), no. 76, 2003; "Les mots désuets" ("Old-fashioned

Words"), no. 48, 1996; "Chambre 28" ("Room 28"), no. 28; "Tous les jardins, tous les parcs" ("All the Gardens, All the Parks"), no. 50, 1997.

Siècle 21 (Paris): "Un rire" ("A Certain Laugh"), no. 9, 2006.

Voix parallèles/Parallel Voices (XYZ éditeur, Montréal, and Quarry Press, Kingston): "Ailleurs, New York" ("Somewhere Else, New York"), 1993.

La maison du rêve (l'Hexagone, Montréal): "La vie rêvée" ("Dream Worlds"), 2000.

Lieux d'être (France): "Funérailles" ("Funeral"), under the title "La petite fille," no. 28, 1999.

Revue de la maison de la poésie Rhône-Alpes (France): "Le chat" ("The Cat"), no. 8, 1990.

Tessera (Toronto): "Une bouteille à la mer" ("A Bottle in the Sea"), vol. 33–34, Winter 2003.

In English translation:

Matrix (Montréal): "Travelling Back" ("Le retour"), no. 60, 2001 (Tr.: Liedewy Hawke).

Catalogue of *Artefact Montréal 2007: Sculptures urbaines/Urban Sculptures*, (on the theme of Expo 67) (Montréal): "A Happy Babel" ("Babel heureuse"), Centre d'art public, 2008 (Tr.: Janet Logan).

Voix parallèles/Parallel Voices (XYZ éditeur, Montréal, and Quarry Press, Kingston): "Elsewhere, New York" ("Ailleurs, New York"), 1993 (Tr.: Ann Diamond).

In Dutch translation:

Vonken van vrijheid (Uitgeverij de Geus, Breda, the Netherlands): "Bevroren lippen" ("Les yeux givrés"), 1995 (Tr.: Marianne Gossije).

In Spanish translation:

Días de Quebec: Antologia de cuentos del Quebec contemporáneo (Conaculta Fonca, Mexico): "Todos los jardines, todos los parques" ("Tous les jardins, tous les parcs"), 2003 (Trad.: Félix Cortés Schöler).

ENVIRONMENTAL BENEFITS STATEMENT

Cormorant Books saved the following resources by printing the pages of this book on chlorine free paper made with 100% post-consumer waste.

TREES	WATER	SOLID WASTE	GREENHOUSE GASES
4	1,801	109	374
FULLY GROWN	GALLONS	POUNDS	POUNDS

Calculations based on research by Environmental Defense and the Paper Task Force.
Manufactured at Friesens Corporation